PENGUIN CRIME FICTION

PRIESTLY MURDERS

Joe Gash is a native of Chicago and a veteran journalist and columnist. Under a different name he is the author of a bestselling series of spy thrillers.

PRIESTLY MURDERS

A Chicago Police Mystery

JOE GASH

PENGUIN BOOKS

To Beverly

PENGUIN BOOKS
Viking Penguin Inc., 40 West 23rd Street,
New York, New York 10010, U.S.A.
Penguin Books Ltd, Harmondsworth,
Middlesex, England
Penguin Books Australia Ltd, Ringwood,
Victoria, Australia
Penguin Books Canada Limited, 2801 John Street,
Markham, Ontario, Canada L3R 1B4
Penguin Books (N.Z.) Ltd, 182–190 Wairau Road,
Auckland 10, New Zealand

First published in the United States of America by
Holt, Rinehart and Winston 1984
Published in Penguin Books by arrangement with
Holt, Rinehart and Winston 1985

LIBRARY OF CONGRESS CATALOGING IN PUBLICATION DATA
Gash, Joe.
   Priestly murders.
   I. Title.
[PS3557.A8446P7   1985]   813'.54   85-9256
ISBN 0 14 00.8223 9

Printed in the United States of America by
George Banta Co., Inc., Harrisonburg, Virginia
Set in Garamond

"Gentlemen, get it straight: The policeman is not there to create disorder. The policeman is there to preserve disorder."
—Richard J. Daley

Author's Note

This book is set in Chicago. It reflects certain realities about the criminal-justice system in that city. The system is not unique to Chicago, however; it works much the same way in all large American cities.

This book—though written before the recent federal investigation of the criminal-justice system in Cook County in which it is alleged by the government that judges, lawyers, and court personnel fixed cases—speaks frankly about deals in court and rushes to indictment and judgment.

The Cook County courts system is the largest in the country. As a result, the unified office of Cook County state's attorney is the largest prosecutor's office in the country. The state's attorney is elected to his position; all ranks below him in the office are a matter of appointment. The First Assistant is second in command followed by the divided commands of the Civil Division and the Criminal Division.

Though there is no permanent Special Squad in the Chicago Police Department's Homicide/Rape Division, such special squads have been set up from time to time to deal with those cases that have excited unusual public interest or special interests on the parts of powerful groups in the city.

As part of a court-mandated affirmative-action program, large numbers of minority candidates for the Chicago Police Department were sworn into service as Chicago policemen without full background checks, according to officers who were assigned to carry out those background checks. This fact is reflected in this book. It is also true that no policeman in Chicago has been discovered to have hidden a previous felony record.

The affirmative-action hiring program in the Chicago Police Department created inevitable animosity between newly hired black officers and veteran white officers (and some veteran black officers who resented the newcomers). This book is not an attempt to explain the black/white problems inside the police department or the attitudes of various members of the criminal-justice system toward black officers or suspects. It is, again, merely a reflection of the actual divisions within the department at the time portrayed in this book.

The Chicago Democratic political organization has controlled the Chicago Police Department at all levels since 1931, despite the use of civil service rules to protect the job security of all ranks. The situation remains unchanged to this day. Thus, certain police actions are dictated in part by political considerations. This situation is not unique to Chicago.

The language used in dialogue in this book accurately reflects the speech of policemen, prosecutors, and street people. It may be offensive to some readers. No gratuitous attempt to shock readers was intended. The book is meant to be a graphic record of the reality of police work without limiting the voice of that reality.

Some terminology used may be unfamiliar to those not acquainted with the criminal-justice system or with some speech peculiarities in Chicago:

Chinaman is a Chicagoism for political sponsor, the equivalent of "rabbi" used in New York City in the same context.

The *star* is the Chicago police word for a badge. *Baton* is the police word for a nightstick. A *squadrol* is a paddy wagon; a *squad* is a marked police car.

The Man on Five, the Boss, and "from the Fifth Floor" are all common references to the Mayor of Chicago, whose office is located on the fifth floor of City Hall.

PRIESTLY
MURDERS

1

THE MASS IS ENDED

They came in the gloom of the rain, shortly after dawn. The sky was sealed with mourning clouds. Two women who had attended the seven o'clock Mass for twenty years came from opposite ends of the street. They nearly met at the steps of St. Alma's Church. As always, they glanced at each other for a moment and nodded in recognition, but did not speak. And then they went their separate ways, the woman in a black coat through the left-hand doors and the woman in a tan coat through the doors on the right. They did not know each other and never spoke, but in twenty years they had become rituals for each other.

The old major who had commanded an infantry company in the Second World War was next, a man of failing health, tottering across Forty-seventh Street with his thin weight resting on a walking stick. He was nearly blind, and when the matter of what happened this morning at Mass was discussed, he could say he saw nothing.

At 7:06, Father Michael Doherty, preceded by a sleepy-eyed black child in black cassock and white alb, came through the marble archway that separated the sacristy from the sanctuary of the old church.

He walked to the modern, slab-sided altar set in the middle of the sanctuary, apart from the old, unused marble high altar. He put down the chalice and kissed the altar stone and began the modern ritual of the ancient Mass.

Father Doherty was as sleepy-eyed as the child who assisted him, which is why the Mass was begun seven minutes late. If he had begun on time, there was a good chance that he would have been alive for breakfast with the old pastor at nine.

"I will go unto the altar of God . . ." he said loudly, and his thin voice echoed curiously down the darkened nave of the church. Above his head and behind him was a huge stained-glass window filled with angels assisting fallen soldiers to a rendezvous with God. The window, as the old pastor had pointed out to Father Doherty, had been commissioned when the parish was wealthy, in the days after World War I, when so many young men of the area had fallen in battle. The history lesson had been accepted quietly by Father Doherty on that first day, but it had not interested him.

He spread his hands and began the long oration of prayers leading to the central moment of the Mass, when

2

Catholics believe that bread and wine are transformed into the body and blood of Christ.

Lightning suddenly cracked across the gloomy sky outside the church and illuminated the stained-glass windows. The few lights in the sanctuary flickered for a moment and then surged with power again.

The old woman on the left-hand side of the church was absorbed in her rosary. She said the rosary during the Mass because she did not like the Mass anymore, though piety demanded her attendance at the rite. The form of ritual had been changed after the reforms of the Second Vatican Council. The Mass had become more communal and was offered in English. Hence the new altar, with the priest in a position to face the congregation, instead of turned away from the congregation as in the old days.

Her name was Margaret Ford and she was seventy-six. She detested the changes. She had always found comfort in the old rituals, in the Latin incantations that stirred her imagination to thoughts of God and angels.

Father Michael Doherty held up the white piece of unleavened bread, and the altar boy, whose name was Clarence Washington, tinkled a small bell. It was the central moment of the Mass.

Father Doherty was thirty-one, two years younger than the man he had come to replace for four weeks. He should have been on vacation, but he had consented to cancel his plans and to serve in dismal St. Alma's parish, at the edge of the black ghetto of the South Side. It was politic to do so; the request had come from his chief chinaman inside the chancery office downtown, Monsignor Culley.

The priest raised the chalice before him, and again Clarence Washington rang the bell. It made a small sound in the huge, darkened silence of the Gothic church.

"This is My Blood, which shall be shed for you and for many," the priest said softly, so softly that the old retired army major could scarcely hear him.

In that moment, Father Doherty thought of himself with pity. Each morning for two weeks—and there were two weeks yet to go—he had dragged himself across the small courtyard from the faded rectory building and through the side entrance of St. Alma's parish church. It was a far cry from the splendor of St. Osmond's Church, on the far Northwest Side, where he was in residence as an assistant. Old St. Alma's had seen its best days. There was speculation that the Archdiocese would close the place down in the fall unless there was a turn in fortunes at the collection plate. The church was damp and drafty and cold, and it cost too much to heat during the long Chicago winters. The roof needed repairs and while the roof was insured—the repairs had been necessitated by snow damage during a severe winter three years before—the people in the chancery office who decided these matters wondered if the money could be better spent elsewhere.

Father Doherty knew these matters because his sponsor in church politics, Monsignor Culley, had told him.

"It would be a favor to me as well as to poor old Mike Hogan at St. Alma's," Monsignor Culley had said to Michael Doherty when asking him to substitute at the church. Mike Hogan was the old pastor and a classmate of Monsignor Culley at the seminary; Hogan had not prospered, but he accepted his lot as a poor parish priest and did not resent Culley's obvious advancement in Church politics. The gentle implications of Culley's request were clear to both men, and Doherty had not hesitated to agree.

The problem had come up because Bill Conklin had moved out of the rectory for the summer.

In the middle of his worship, Father Doherty frowned at the thought of Bill Conklin. It was only a moment, but it was deeply felt. He had never liked Bill Conklin very much anyway, and now Conklin had arrogantly decided to ruin Doherty's summer—even without realizing it.

"Lord, I am not worthy that You should come to me; say the Word and my soul shall be healed." Father Doherty held a small host before him and repeated the words three times and then descended three marble steps to the old-fashioned marble altar rail to dispense Holy Communion.

The old major shuffled forward and stood before the rail. It was too difficult for him to kneel anymore, and he felt ashamed of his infirmity. His red-blotched face was turned vaguely in the direction of the blurred image of the young priest coming to him. The major closed his eyes to receive his Lord.

The other two were at the Communion rail as well. The woman named Margaret Ford, in the black coat, stood on the left side of the major, and the woman named Helen Wilson, in the tan coat, stood on the major's right.

The Three Musketeers, Father Michael Doherty thought with a smile. Always the same, every morning, year after year. How sad and dreadful and beautiful, he thought, shivering at the twin images of age and faith. Michael Doherty was proud of his insight in that moment; he had always considered himself a man of delicate sensibilities.

The old women knelt—a further humiliation to the standing major—and opened their mouths and closed their eyes to receive Communion in the old-fashioned way, before the Church reforms had permitted them to accept the host from the priest in their hands.

Michael Doherty gave Communion to Helen Wilson and then to the major and then to Margaret Ford and automatically turned to go back to the altar. But Clarence Washington, who was nine, saw what Father Doherty did not see and had already started along the altar rail, with the brass-plated paten in his hand, to a fourth figure.

Michael Doherty turned back, somewhat annoyed, and then thought: I'm packing them in. I'll have to boast to the pastor at breakfast. He smiled to himself.

In that moment he thought of breakfast and of the old man and of Father Bill Conklin and of the benign sponsorship of Monsignor Culley at the chancery office and of his own chances of advancement in the hierarchy in the years to come. He thought of all these mixed things as another flash of thunder eerily illuminated the interior of the darkened, damp church. He saw the fourth figure, dressed in a police uniform, wearing the black leather patrol jacket half-opened, pinned with a five-pointed shield that the Chicago police called a "star." Coming home off patrol, Michael Doherty thought with amusement, a good Catholic boy.

But something was not quite right.

The priest crossed the main aisle on the altar side of the Communion rail—in the area called the sanctuary—and simultaneously reached inside the chalice for another disk of the unleavened white bread baked by an order of nuns in a Chicago suburb and sold to the Archdiocese in huge amounts that afforded the nuns a comfortable life-style.

Something was not right, his brain repeated, and he saw what it was.

The policeman still wore his helmet.

A baby-blue, egg-shaped helmet with the outline of a star painted on the front and the unnecessary words CHICAGO POLICE in an arc above the painted star.

Why would he wear his helmet in church?

The priest stopped and frowned, and Clarence Washington, unaware that Doherty had stopped, continued three steps forward, which separated him from the body of the priest.

Perhaps it was all the fourth figure had been waiting for.

Now, as the two old women rose creakily to their feet from the rubber kneeler at the rail, as the major steadied himself with a thin white hand on the back of the first pew, as Clarence Washington turned back to Father Doherty, the fourth figure pulled a small pistol from his belt and fired.

The first bullet struck Father Doherty in the center of the forehead and burned an ashen hole between his wide, startled eyes. He was dead even as the chalice struck the floor and the hosts were scattered across the marble. But he remained on his feet for a moment, and a second shot

7

plunged a pellet into his chest. It was unnecessary.

Lightning forked the sky again and a surge of light crashed against the stained-glass windows. Clarence Washington, who stood absolutely still, stared at Father Michael Doherty as he sank slowly to his knees as though in prayer and then fell forward, his forehead striking the marble. And then Clarence, who was terrified, suddenly knelt as well—not to aid the priest, but to gather up the spilled hosts on the floor. The hosts had been consecrated; the hosts contained the essence of Christ. These thoughts numbly pushed aside the reality of the dead priest as Clarence Washington took the hosts, one by one, and placed them in the chalice.

The fourth figure stared at the back of the boy as though deciding something, and then the gun disappeared somewhere in his belt. The policeman turned and walked quickly down the darkened aisle to the rear of the church.

For a long moment, there was only the sound of the two shots still reverberating in the vast emptiness of the church and then the sound of heels tapping along the linoleum aisle to the door at the back of the church. And when the door slammed shut at the back of the church, there was no other sound but a long, threatening peal of thunder. And then a streak of lightning made the lamps in the church surge again and then fade. A pool of blood spread slowly from the body of the priest and touched the unleavened bread near him, and Clarence Washington reached for the piece of bread and reverently replaced it in the chalice.

2

A CHINAMAN'S CHANCE

Sergeant Terry Flynn felt uncomfortable. He wiped one freckled hand across his wide, square Irish features and then repeated the gesture, as though attempting to wash away the scene before him.

It was still raining. It always was raining, Terry Flynn thought. It had been a wet summer and now it was a wet fall and he thought, not for the first time in the past four years, that he would be happier as a security guard someplace in Southern California. A sign of creeping senility, Lieutenant Schmidt would have said with a smile, but Terry Flynn really meant it this morning.

The beat cop from the district had arrived on the scene nineteen minutes after the murder. In the confused moments after his arrival in the church—suddenly lighted front to back on orders of the old pastor, Father Hogan, as though to chase death from the place—the beat cop had wallowed in the wildly divergent accounts of the four eyewitnesses to the crime.

Homicide was called in twenty-three minutes after the murder, and the decision to assign someone from the Special Squad was made at the deputy-superintendent level forty minutes after the murder. The Homicide detectives from Area Two on the South Side resented the appearance of Flynn from the Special Squad the moment he came into the church through the front doors. Terry Flynn didn't blame them.

The beat cop was named Hourihan and he was only twenty-five years old. This was his eighth homicide in two years on the job. He was in a busy district of the city, encompassing some of the rougher parts of the ghetto. The sight of the dead man did not bother him more than the sight of the other dead he had seen; later, at home, in the normalcy of his surroundings in the Southwest Side bungalow on which he held the mortgage, the murder would come again to mind, but it would be too bizarre to contemplate, as though it were something that had happened long ago.

"So we got two say it was a cop and one says it was some black guy and one who says he didn't see nothing. Right?" asked Terry Flynn, and for a moment no one replied. The coroner's man was on his knees at the side of the body, running his fingers carefully over the vestments. His name was Caffrey and he had been at it so long that he felt more comfortable with the dead than with the living. His gentle fingers turned the priest's head slightly and he saw the wound and touched it.

"Yeah, the usual clear and accurate account of the incident that we always get," said Hauptmann at last. He was the Homicide detective from Area Two. "I figure the two old ladies were too far away to see much anyway. The pastor here, his name is Mike Hogan, he turned on all the lights."

"It wasn't like this when the hit came?" asked Terry Flynn.

"No. Dark as the neighborhood," said Hauptmann. "We had the old priest turn the lights on so we could see around the body. When the hit came, the dead man dropped his cup, what do you call that thing?"

"A chalice, you Protestant bastard," said his partner, Detective John Kelly. "I don't even see why they let people like you on the force."

Hauptmann grinned then, as though both of them wanted lightness, like the moment when the old priest had erased the gloom of the church by turning on all the lights. Hauptmann and Kelly had been together for a long time in Homicide, and some of the things they had seen were fairly bad. But the matter of a priest killed in the middle of worship had frightened them into longing to treat the matter more lightly.

Sergeant Flynn thought he understood it, and said nothing for a moment.

Then he resumed, "So you put your money on the kid?"

"I don't bet on this one. The kid had his back turned when the hit went down and he stayed that way and then dropped to the floor to grab up the . . . the . . ." Hauptmann hesitated and looked at John Kelly.

11

Kelly whispered loudly, "Communion wafers. The hosts."

"Yeah. But he was in front of the dead man when the dead man was coming across the aisle, from there over to here, to give Communion, and the kid says it was a poh-leese man."

"You running a check on the kid?"

"Sure, but we just got here. He's got a home, lives with his mother, she's divorced. I get this from the kid. He say he ain't never been in no trouble, oss-if-fer," Hauptmann said, lapsing into the standard urban black dialect that cops use to mimic the speech of blacks.

"I didn't think you could still get kids to get up at seven to serve Mass," Sergeant Terry Flynn said, and watched Caffrey's hands finish their spiderlike probing of the body. He thought of Terry Flynn growing up on the South Side, in this same parish, when the neighborhood was white and Irish, awakening at sunrise and going down the streets colored blood-red by dawn to this church to serve 6:00 A.M. Mass. For a moment Terry Flynn turned his face toward the old marble altar, no longer used, and tried to think of himself as he had been then, and of this church as it had been. But it was no use. It had been a long time and he hadn't seen the inside of this church or any other for a lot of years.

The church seemed smaller to him because he had always seen it with a child's perspective in the past, and later in memory, which made the past seem mythically huge. He had lived in a world of giants when he was a child, and could not understand he had grown to a giant himself.

12

This was a very bad killing, he thought, and he wished he had Lieutenant Schmidt to guide him. Schmidt was his mentor without meaning to be so, and Terry Flynn felt lost with Schmidt away on vacation leave. Matt Schmidt and Gert were in Europe again. Probably going through churches, Flynn thought.

"Look, you guys could handle this as good as anybody, and I don't like breaking in any more than you do. But the deputy got an ant up his ass when he heard it was a priest got hit, and then when he gets wind that a cop was involved, he doesn't want to touch it. He bucks it to us so that we can fuck it up," Terry Flynn said in his gravelly voice. Matthew Schmidt would say he was turning on the charm.

"Listen, I don't give a fuck either," said Hauptmann. "I don't like to get involved in things that get too much interest downtown. I like my retirement out here, I like shine murders. You solve them by beating the shit out of the guy you know did it and that's satisfaction. I don't want to go headhunting for some rogue in the department."

"Guys, watch your language," said John Kelly softly. He had taken to whispering as soon as they entered the church, and when Hauptmann expressed amusement at this, John Kelly had felt embarrassed. He did not count himself as a Catholic anymore—he would have said he was "fallen away"—but certain shibboleths of childhood were engraved too deeply on his conscience to be changed by mere middle age or lack of faith. You didn't use bad language in church.

Flynn smiled at the injunction and then walked across

13

the marble to the place where Father Michael Doherty, thirty-one, had fallen. The witnesses and the church janitor and the pastor were all waiting for the police in the sitting room of the rectory, away from the crime. Kelly had decided on that because it was obvious that the murder scene was upsetting to them. The old women were deep in shock and the major was rambling on about war, and the altar boy, Clarence Washington, sat in his cassock and surplice, staring at his hands on his lap, his eyes very wide. It was better for them not to be here. Besides, it was better if none of them saw the way police worked a scene.

"The scene" was what the Homicide men called it, and it was a holy moment in the aftermath of a crime. Detectives had an instinctive faith that the scene held the ultimate clue to the solution of the murder, and they were reluctant to close it. Detectives, medical examiners (as the younger coroners now called themselves), police photographers, uniformed men—all milled around the edges of the scene, trying to understand what they were certain was an obvious fact that would make the murder solvable.

"What have you got?" Terry Flynn said, going down on one knee beside Caffrey. Caffrey smelled of formaldehyde and death. He was a thin man with crafty gray eyes and a dislike for too much speech. It was part of his increasing phobia about the company of living men.

"Well, it looks like two, so far. This one"—he turned the head of the body again and exposed the blackened, neat, bloodless wound in the forehead—"and one down in the gut. I can turn him over—"

"I'll take your word," said Terry Flynn. "Small piece."

"Yeah. I'd say a .22. Very pro. The slug rolled around inside him, the second one, but I'll bet a dime to a donut the slug in the head was first and was the one that killed him."

"Why?"

Caffrey looked at the heavyset Irishman next to him with genuine loathing—not for the question, which was a part of his job, but for his physical proximity. Terry Flynn smelled of sweating flesh, smelled of cigarettes and a morning beer, of foul human life. In death, corpses took on a sweet odor of putrefaction that Caffrey could clean away, reducing the complex to simple parts, numbering the organs of the body like so many bits of a puzzle to be taken apart.

"In the center, dead on. If the shooter had put one in his gut with the first shot, I doubt he would have decided to go for the head with the second. I also doubt that he would have got it dead on. There doesn't appear to be any angle of entry, like if the priest was falling forward or something."

"So the shooter thinks he's Deadeye Dick, going for the brain with shot number one."

"It could be chance, it might be like you say. A .22 isn't the best piece for a head shot. Remember that Jap in the Outfit got hit three or four times in the head by a hit man? And lived?"

"Gooks got hard heads," Terry Flynn said.

"Everybody's got a hard head, that's why God made skulls. This head shot could have just as easy bounced off, too. If he had used a silencer, which would have cut down the velocity of the slug, or if the shooter had been even twenty feet further back, there's a good chance our friend wouldn't be dead."

Flynn stood up and his knees cracked noisily. The constant rain had made him feel a touch rheumatic over the past month but he had spoken about it to no one. Except to Karen Kovac, who was also in the Special Squad.

Thinking of Karen Kovac seemed out of place, even though she was a Homicide detective as well. Terry Flynn frowned and turned. He knew what it was. It was the church, the place where he had been a child, where he had learned the church lessons of life and death and resurrection, of sin and hell. He had been a Catholic and so had Karen, but a lot of life had intervened since their childhood days. Terry Flynn had a war to remember and a bad marriage; Karen Kovac had a marriage that had failed and a sort of keen bitterness at the way life was turning out. They had become lovers and everyone knew about it because nothing is secret.

Lieutenant Matthew Schmidt had once considered separating them from the Squad for a while, but then decided to divide the work schedule so that they were rarely together on the job. This suited both of them because, oddly, they did not work very well together.

"Who was this guy, anyway?" Terry Flynn said at last to the two homicide detectives.

"Well, this wasn't his regular parish, for one thing. He came from St. Osmond's to fill in for some priest who

16

had taken a vacation or something," John Kelly said. "He's got a chinaman down at the chancery office, some guy named Monsignor Culley, and Culley transfers him up here to help the old pastor, this guy Hogan, out of a squeeze. This parish is not going downhill, this parish is in the toilet. These three witnesses are old whites, still living where they lived when St. Alma's was as white as you are. Poor old bastards, imagine having to live around here. You know—"

"I grew up in the parish," said Terry Flynn.

"Yeah?" said John Kelly. The remark made him stop for a moment, as if embarrassed by the idea that Flynn could have some personal connection with the scene in the church. He looked around. "Nice church," he said finally. "These old buildings. Too bad it— Well, they could fix it up, you know?"

"Yeah," Terry Flynn said. "A little paint can do wonders. So, about this priest—"

"Well, this guy Doherty has a lot of ambition—I'm getting this now from the old pastor, he's a sharp old dude—and he says when Doherty's chinaman, who happens to be an old pal of Hogan, says jump, then Doherty jumps. So he wasn't even supposed to be here today, you might say."

"Well, what the hell is the motive?" said Terry Flynn.

"Beats the shit out of me," said Hauptmann. "I checked the poor boxes, though you don't have to waste a priest to steal from a poor box. They ain't got no poor boxes, the old priest says. The poor boxes were ripped off a long time ago, so now all they got is poor people and not too many of them. They're going to close this parish up, I think. Nice-looking church, huh?"

Terry Flynn said nothing but stared at the vast arches buttressing the ceiling.

John Kelly said, "I don't figure a cop. I don't figure it. Maybe a security guard dressed like a cop—"

Hauptmann interrupted. "The kid says he's wearing an eggshell, and security guards don't do that."

"So maybe the kid is wrong, maybe he thinks he saw an eggshell because he sees three-wheeler cowboys every day," John Kelly said.

"And maybe it's a cop," Terry Flynn said, and the three men were silent for a moment. It was dirty enough to have a priest wasted in church. There would be enough heat for everyone. But if it was a cop . . .

"I want to close this guy," Caffrey said at last.

Terry Flynn frowned. He felt too lost. The scene was finished but he was reluctant to close it. Finally he nodded and two uniformed men threw down a body bag and lifted the remains of Michael Doherty and deposited them gently inside the bag and zipped it shut. The two policemen then placed the body bag on a stretcher and lifted it. A pool of drying blood lay on the marble floor and formed a small waterfall down the steps to the Communion rail.

"It still raining outside?" asked one of the uniforms.

"When I came in, it was," said Terry Flynn.

"Shit," said the uniform.

Exactly, Terry Flynn thought. Exactly.

3
ONE OF OUR OWN

The chief of Homicide glared at Sergeant Terry Flynn from behind his large desk on the sixth floor of police headquarters at Eleventh and State. It was nearly noon and Terry Flynn felt hungry for lunch and thirsty for a beer, but Leonard Ranallo was not going to let him leave so easily.

The murder was nearly five hours old and it was as confusing now as it had been the moment he had been called in on the case. He didn't like it—the feel of the case, the raw, wet day, the rumbling in his stomach which annoyed him even more than it annoyed Commander Ranallo.

"I should have been called into the scene, you know that, what the fuck are you doing behind my back?" Ranallo said for the second time in five minutes.

"Look, I don't really want this any more than I want

a hole in the head," Terry Flynn said. "The two guys out of Area Two could handle this just as well as me, but I was called down on it by the deputy, so what am I going to do about it?"

"That motherfucker Nimrod," said Ranallo of the deputy superintendent who had assigned someone from Special Squad to the matter.

It was all politics, as Lieutenant Schmidt might have explained gently to Terry Flynn, and it didn't matter. Ranallo hated the idea of Special Squad because it took attention away from his own leadership of Homicide. It might be pointed out by some in the detective division that Leonard Ranallo could not lead his way out of a paper bag, but it would not have mattered to Ranallo, who put down any scorn to professional jealousy.

Leonard Ranallo was ambitious and a great favorite of the local media, and he intended to remain a favorite by inserting himself from time to time in spectacular cases and then feeding inside information to the reporters. In the parlance of the Chicago Police Department, Ranallo was a wiener, but Leonard Ranallo would have been the last person to know it.

"You talk to the reporters yet?"

Terry Flynn shook his head.

"You sure?"

"The papers didn't tumble to it right away, they been leaving the police uncovered early in the morning, so I was gone from St. Alma's before the press showed up."

"You know a lot about how the papers work?" Ranallo said with a tinge of jealousy.

20

"I know what I know," Terry Flynn said. He was getting a little tired of it and there was an edge to his voice. When it came down to it, Terry Flynn did not let anyone push him around for long, which made it surprising that he had made sergeant at all.

"I'll issue the statements on this case, Flynn," Ranallo said. "I'll talk to the media when they need something. I don't want nothing on this case coming out of Special Squad."

"I got no time to talk to reporters, I gotta work for a living," said Terry Flynn.

"What does that mean, Sergeant? You jacking me around or what?"

"It means it's five hours since the priest was wasted, and I got more work than I know what to do with. I called up Sid Margolies at home and asked him to come down on this."

"This is a lousy one, you know that. We got enough problems without someone thinking cops go around wasting priests in church."

"Tell me about it."

Ranallo softened. Flynn wasn't going to be a problem, he decided. There were plenty of opportunities in a thing like this, plenty of ways to make the publicity work for you, so long as you handled it right.

"I want that cop, I don't care who you got to step on to get that cop," Ranallo said.

"If he is a cop."

"If that's going to be your attitude, maybe I should get someone else—"

Flynn flushed and suddenly slammed a meaty fist on the desk of the Commander of Homicide. Ranallo was startled by the gesture and the sound of the fist on department-issue desk metal.

"I ain't got no fucking attitude and you got no fucking right to say anything like that to me and I don't give a fuck who the fuck you are. I got one nine-year-old shine eyewitness who says he saw a cop and then didn't see him waste a priest and the kid is shook up and don't know what the fuck he saw. Maybe he saw a security dick or maybe he saw a bus driver or maybe he didn't see nothing. I got a blind old man who *really* didn't see nothing and two old biddies who get mixed up every time they open their mouths. So who killed who? And why kill a priest? And why waste him right there in church? What the hell is the motive? Zero. Zip. Except there was one because we got one dead young man. So don't you give me crap about my fucking attitude. I ain't a head-hunter and I don't cover up. If I can clear this fucking thing no matter if it turns out to be the Mayor's son who did it, nothing gives me more pleasure except not talking to you about my fucking attitude."

There was silence for a long moment, broken only by the squeal of an elevated train below the windows of Ranallo's office. The train turned tortuously along the double dip from the South Side and began the mournful journey around the eastern edge of the Loop to the tracks leading to the West Side. It was raining pitilessly and Ranallo's two windows were open to catch the damp slight breeze.

"I'm going to forget you said that. Nothing is going to leave this office, Flynn," Ranallo said after a moment. "You're a good dick, I know that, I worked with you."

You never worked with me in your life except to fuck up an investigation, Terry Flynn thought, but he said nothing. Perhaps three years ago he would have spoken his thought aloud. Some of Matthew Schmidt's persistence in wearing down his rough edges was beginning to pay off.

"You do what you got to do and you get who you got to get and you report to me and I want a report every morning. I'll take the heat for you, from anyone, from the Mayor or the superintendent or the media. Don't worry, I'll give you all the support you need, you know I stand behind you," Leonard Ranallo said, and his narrow Italian face broke into a smile of good fellowship so false that Terry Flynn had to smile in return.

"Yeah, I know," Flynn said. "I shouldn't pop off."

"Forget it. You get out there and you kick ass. I want this one and if it turns out it's one of ours, then let the chips fall where they may. I got to go up and brief the superintendent now. Where you headed now?"

"I got to link up with Sid Margolies," Terry Flynn said. "Then we got to go to St. Osmond's where Doherty was from and try to figure out why someone wanted to kill him."

"Killing a priest," said Ranallo. "I can't think of anything worse than that."

"Yeah," said Flynn. He could think of worse things he had seen.

"Scum. I can't think of anything worse than that," Ranallo repeated, inventing a sneering face to match his words. He was a showman, even in a private conference. Terry Flynn felt nothing but contempt for him.

"I can," Terry Flynn said softly.

Ranallo dropped the sneer and looked up. "What?"

"A cop killing a priest," said Terry Flynn, and the two men stared at each other for a long moment before Flynn turned and opened the office door and closed it quietly behind him.

4

STEPPING ON TOES

The Archbishop of Chicago sat behind the walnut desk on the second floor of his residence and told the young priest to admit the visitor waiting downstairs.

The rain had stopped for the moment, but the trees in Lincoln Park, across from the residence, stood half-naked and shivering in silent rows, waiting for more of the deluge. The grass was turning brown, and from his window the Archbishop could catch just a glimpse of the gray, ragged edge of Lake Michigan that formed the eastern edge of the five-mile-long park.

The residence was a redstone building of the last century, a mansion with a dozen fireplaces and an old-fashioned circular driveway that led to the covered portico of the entrance. A battered brown Dodge sat in the driveway now. The car carried no special markings except for the

Illinois license number beginning with the letters ZA, which identified it as an unmarked police car. Why some bureaucrat had decided to affix the ZA prefix to police cars that were not supposed to be identified as police cars was one of the mysteries of government never spoken of.

The Archbishop of the wealthiest Catholic diocese in the world had requested the interview through his liaison man inside the chancery.

Normally, Commander Ranallo would have visited His Eminence, but Ranallo had been unreachable all morning, and finally a harassed aide in the superintendent's office had suggested that one of the Special Squad men go. Everyone knew what it was about.

Sid Margolies entered the immense office and stood at the door for a moment, hat in hand, blinking.

Margolies had twenty-two years in the department and sixteen in Homicide. He had never made rank and never expected to. He had no chinamen at the upper department levels because he never cared to cultivate one. He was Jewish and a detective and that combination, while not unusual, was rare enough to single him out. He was a thin, pale man of precise gestures and a certain glum expression that seemed to expect nothing but the worst from the world. He wore that expression now.

"Why don't *you* see him?" he had said to Terry Flynn when Flynn told him of the assignment.

"Because I don't like him," said Terry Flynn.

"You don't like the cardinal? What's he ever done to you?"

"Nothing. I just don't like him."

"I never heard you express an opinion on religion."

26

"I got no opinion, I just don't like the cardinal."

"I don't understand you sometimes," Sid Margolies had said.

"That's because you're Jewish and the Irish are inscrutable to you."

"What do I tell him?"

"Shit. I don't know. What the hell is he going to ask you?"

"Maybe somebody beefed about us."

"Jesus H. Christ, Sid, we're the fucking police investigating a homicide. I got no time for singing and dancing with the hoity-toity about this. Ranallo should be there, not us. He wants to be the wiener in this one. Son of a bitch probably is hiding out because he didn't go to confession last Saturday or something."

It was that kind of a case and it was getting worse.

Terry Flynn had spent three hours at St. Osmond's with Sid Margolies, and they couldn't get a thing out of the priests. Except that Michael Doherty was a fine young man. He came from a fine Catholic family. He was kindly and wise and generous and worked well with everyone and loved children and blah-blah-blah. As Terry Flynn had put it.

Michael Doherty's parents were alive and lived in Winnetka and they had been as much help as the gaggle of priests who could speak no ill of the dead in St. Osmond's. Their Michael had always been a religious boy, always been a paragon of virtue, once when he was twelve he had walked three miles to return an overdue library book and . . .

"Sounds like our man was either Abe Lincoln or Saint

Francis of Assisi," said Terry Flynn, and Sid Margolies had agreed. Their gloom had spread.

Now it was three days after the Monday-morning murder of Michael Doherty in St. Alma's Church. The funeral for the dead priest would be held tomorrow in Holy Name Cathedral on the near North Side, and the Archbishop of Chicago had, in the words of a press release, "decided to celebrate the Mass for our fallen martyr."

The Archbishop of Chicago was a man of immense girth and a large, flat face. He wore the crimson robes this morning and a crimson skullcap. Across his broad belly dangled the pectoral cross that had been given to him in Rome three years before by one of his sponsors in the Vatican. He wore the ring of office on his right hand but he did not extend it to Sid Margolies. It was just as well, because Margolies would not have known what to do about it.

"Sergeant Margolies," began the Cardinal in his curiously small voice.

"It's Detective Margolies," Sid Margolies said. "The head of the unit—acting head—is tied up at the moment and they told me you wanted to talk to someone who was actually involved with the case."

"And you are leading the investigation? I thought Commander Ranallo—"

Margolies saw difficulties with this line of conversation. He wondered if the Cardinal was put out by the appearance of a mere detective instead of someone higher up. Or maybe he was anti-semitic, Margolies thought.

"Commander Ranallo is the head of the investigation,

but we figured you wanted to talk to us, thought maybe you wanted an update—"

"Do you have an update?" the Cardinal asked, extending his right hand to indicate two red plush chairs arranged in front of a fireplace. Margolies took a chair and the Cardinal sat down heavily opposite him. Margolies was surprised to see that a small fire was actually burning in the fireplace, though the room was too warm for it.

"Well, sir," Margolies began and paused, trying to think of the correct form of address.

The Cardinal glanced sharply at him and noticed the puzzlement on his face. For the first time, the large man smiled. "Be comfortable, Detective Margolies. This is informal."

Which, Margolies thought quickly, it was not. "Well, you see, Reverend, the problem with this is that there was no reason for anyone to want to kill Father Doherty."

The slow, insincere smile was replaced quickly by a frown that seemed to come from the heart. "I don't follow you, Detective," the small voice tried to rumble.

"Motive. We don't have any. So we got to assume this is just a crazy act, something that happens once in a while, some guy just becomes crazy and kills someone for no reason."

"Someone who hates priests?"

"Maybe. Or maybe someone who hates cops and kills priests dressed like a cop," said Margolies softly. He noticed the newspapers arrayed on a low coffee table behind him. He had read them all. He liked to read newspapers, but the stories had not been pleasant. The *Chicago Daily News* had brought up recollections of past acts of villainy in the police department to tie to the present "rogue cop." *Chicago Today* had obtained a photograph of the dead priest *in mortis*, and the *Tribune* had suggested that the police department should hire outside investigators to help solve the murder. Margolies had felt sick reading the stories, and had felt sicker when he and Flynn had been called in to brief Ranallo yesterday morning. The superintendent had sent his liaison man to listen in on the briefing. Nobody had liked it when Terry Flynn explained they didn't have a clue to the murder of the priest.

"You have no leads at all," the Cardinal now said, his frown deepening. He sounded as disapproving as Ranallo.

"No. We are working on some matters," Margolies said. For a moment he forgot the room and the fat prelate in the next chair. He made a face that signaled concentration. His dark voice, mild and logical, was trying to explain:

"We are running down personnel sheets on every tactical police officer who might have been in uniform on the South Side within ten hours of the time of the murder. It takes time. If our eyewitness is right, the killer wore a helmet of the sort worn by a three-wheeler officer. But maybe somebody used to be a three-wheeler officer and kept his helmet. It's a lot of men, Reverend, and we got three people borrowed from Area Two on it—"

"I don't understand the internal workings of the police department, but when I talked to the superintendent this morning, I did ask for the people actually involved in this matter to fill me in on their progress," the Cardinal said, letting the word *superintendent* drop so casually that Sid Margolies was bound not to miss it.

Sid Margolies understood. The superintendent had by-passed Ranallo on this to stick it in Ranallo's ass. Except we're the stick. Me, Sid Margolies thought then, I'm the stick and that's why Flynn sent me, to cover his own ass when Ranallo finds out he missed a chance to chat with the Cardinal. It's hard to trust anyone these days, he thought.

"Eminence," Margolies said, his mind tripping finally on the correct form of address, "most murders are simple. There are motives. Guys kill their wives, wives kill their husbands, dope dealers kill other dope dealers because of turf arguments." Sid Margolies paused because the Cardinal was frowning at the elementary lesson in criminology.

Sid Margolies cleared his throat to try again. "But this is a young man who was a priest doing another priest a favor in a parish, and in walks someone that nobody knows, who might have been wearing a police uniform, and he simply assassinates him." Margolies spoke slowly, like a patient teacher. "We're not television cops, Eminence, we don't just 'hit the street' and get information from shoeshine boys. It doesn't work that way in something like this."

"What are you going to do, then?" the Cardinal asked.

"We got to slog it," Margolies said. "Just go down the lists, go down the lists of people like security guards, CTA

31

drivers, just try to figure out if there might have been someone with a hard-on for the parish there or the church. Oh. I beg your pardon."

The Cardinal did not reply.

"Sir, I don't know what you want me to tell you."

"That you have found the person who committed this act," the Cardinal said. "This is a large city, but you have a vast police force. I told the superintendent that I expected no stone unturned."

Sid Margolies frowned but said nothing.

"Mr. Margolies, I can assure you that I have faith in the Chicago Police Department and—"

"I thought of something," Sid Margolies said suddenly, and he had. He had been staring at the fire in the fireplace to avoid the frowning gaze of the Cardinal and he had seen it, tripped into memory by some association of thoughts and words he would not have been able to explain, even to himself.

"The Archdiocese gets threats, right?"

"I beg your pardon?"

"The Church. The Catholic Church. You get threats, right?"

"I'm not aware of it."

Margolies frowned. "Everyone get threats. Newspapers get threats, cops get threats, judges get threats, corporations get threats, neighbors get threats. There are a lot of nuts walking around and they threaten people. They write notes with crayons and things or else they write nice typewritten letters but they're the same kind of nuts. Most of them are nuisances but there might be something

32

there. Maybe somebody threatened the parish, maybe somebody sent a letter here and said he was going to destroy the Catholic Church. Something like that."

There was a long silence between the two men, one in his damp raincoat and dark tie and rain-sweated face, the other in the comfortable and ostentatious robes designed for princes of another age.

"I'm not aware of any threats," said the Cardinal stiffly.

Margolies waited. Something was wrong. He stared at the fat man sitting across from him and he realized the Cardinal's eyes had gone as flat as a cat's.

The Cardinal was lying to him, Sid Margolies thought calmly. For the first time since Terry Flynn had called him into the matter, Sid Margolies felt something was finally happening.

5

TAKE A GIRL LIKE YOU

Karen Kovak wore a white silky kimono and nothing else. She sat at the edge of the couch and poured a glass of wine from a half-full bottle. The kimono opened slightly as she poured but she did nothing to close it. Perhaps she intended to let it open, as she intended nearly everything she did.

She was a slender woman with a beautiful Polish face framed with short blond hair. Her eyes were blue—the clear, cloudless blue eyes of Poles, without brooding behind the color of them. The brooding, when it came, formed itself on her thin lips, around a wide mouth. She was very pretty in an unconventional way, and she had always thought she was not so pretty as all that.

Terry Flynn sat at the opposite end of the couch and stared at her and saw her breasts revealed and then accepted the glass of wine from her and smiled. He was not a wine drinker because he had no real sophistication. Or so he often bragged. Karen Kovac had changed some of that because Terry Flynn had wanted to please her.

"Now what is this stuff? French or what?" He said it to please her; he didn't really care. He wished he were drinking a can of cold beer.

"California. A very good zinfandel," Karen Kovac said. She sipped the wine and Terry Flynn said, "Salut," and took a swallow of his own.

Raining again, the fourth day of that week. The sewers had backed up in several hundred basements in the suburbs and on the South Side and the newscaster at ten o'clock said Salt Creek was overflowing, spilling into the yards of hundreds of homes in the near western suburbs.

Terry Flynn had come to her apartment drenched. His tan trench coat had been nearly black with wetness. His face had been flushed and covered with moisture. He had looked so miserable and cold that Karen changed her mind about their date. They would stay home, they would share a platter of linguine with clam sauce and share a bottle of wine and then they would make love to each other. They did not speak of making love to each other. All their lovemaking was silent, even before, especially after. It was as though their relationship was too fragile for words.

They both had come to feel that good things in life were easily broken.

"I thought you told me a good policeman never gets wet," Karen Kovac had said to him with a smile as he took off his dripping trench coat. His blond hair was plastered against his scalp. His nose was red and he sneezed at first in answer, and Karen Kovac laughed, though not unkindly.

"That was my father," he said. Terry Flynn came from a cop family. His father had been a clout-heavy commander in the old days in the department and when he retired, he went to Florida with satisfied cynicism and a large bank account—the world was as corrupt and bad as he had expected it to be, and he had profited by it. Terry Flynn never knew why he had followed his father into the force, because they shared few ideals about the job—or, rather, Terry Flynn had a few, whereas his father had had none.

He had taken a long shower while she prepared supper. Her son, her only child by her disastrous marriage, was staying overnight at a friend's house. It was Friday and there was no school tomorrow.

When he emerged from the shower with a large blue kimono wrapped around his heavy frame, he joined her in the small kitchen and sat at the table drinking wine while she chopped vegetables into a pan.

"This is a lot better idea than going to Second City," Terry Flynn said.

"You want a cheap date," she said, her back to him.

"No. I just want you, not a bunch of people trying to be funny on a stage."

"You looked like a wet dog when you came in," she said.

"I smelled like one, too," he said. "We've been going

fourteen hours a day on this thing. You can't rub the stink off when you work like that."

She said nothing for a moment. They usually tried not to talk about the job, but it was difficult. Policemen talk to other policemen because there is an instinctive feeling that no one else can understand what it is to do the job. And there is another feeling, too—a feeling that you have to have a life outside of the work, untainted by the ugliness and the toughness of it or even by the strange occasional satisfaction of a break in a case. It is the reason why policemen rarely tell their wives what they do during the day. Karen Kovac had once said that to him with a trace of bitterness. Both had been married before, but Terry Flynn had had the policeman's wife; they had divorced because Terry Flynn ended up having nothing to say to her.

"Are you getting anyplace?"

"No. Sid had a bright idea yesterday but it isn't working out. He figured some nut was threatening the Church. It wasn't much but it was something. But the Cardinal panned that idea. The problem is that Matt Schmidt isn't here, that's the problem. I can't deal with Ranallo and with the fucking superintendent sending down his gofer twice a day for little chats. Matt could run the interference."

"Matt won't be back for another week."

Terry Flynn lit a Lucky Strike and stared at the glass of wine as though it were a glass of beer. The act of concentration did not work. He picked up the glass of wine and took another sip. It was still wine.

"I'm not cut out to be an executive or an ass-kisser," he said.

"Aren't you?" she said and smiled at him and he felt pleased suddenly, as though for one moment they had decided to really speak to each other, not about other things but about themselves. But then he flushed, and in a moment the silence between them pushed them apart again. Terry Flynn was a loud, aggressive man whose sudden silences betrayed a certain shy confusion over what he should say next. It was a childlike quality, and perhaps it was one that endeared him to Karen Kovac, who always knew what she wanted to say.

"Not an executive, anyway. With your ass, I'll make an exception," he managed at last and tried on a smile.

"What does Sid make of this? I mean, all of it?"

"You mean because he's Jewish and it's all Catholic stuff? He's as lost as I am. He met the Cardinal. He doesn't like him either. There's a lot of heat on this and I can't count on Ranallo to back us up. I wish to Christ Matt was here."

"You said that," Karen Kovac said, and she realized how miserable Terry Flynn was. What attracted her to him was what held her back from him as well. He was blunt and honest in his way, but he was truly unable to comprehend how to deal politically inside the department. He had made sergeant on a fluke and on the belated influence of his old man; he would never be more. That saddened her and yet thrilled her as well because she intended to be much, much more. The knowledge always kept a gulf between them, though Terry Flynn did not understand it.

They had met when Karen Kovac, an ordinary patrol officer, had been inducted into the Special Squad on temporary duty as a decoy to catch a man who had been killing blondes. The fact that the decoy operation succeeded, though she was nearly the fourth victim of the killer, had decided Matt Schmidt to recommend her for permanent status as a Homicide detective. She had passed the detective's examination easily and been assigned to Schmidt's Special Squad. But before that, she had become Terry Flynn's lover for no reason at all except she liked him. Perhaps she even loved him, though she would not have said that to anyone. Least of all to Terry Flynn.

Suddenly she felt bad about him and thought of him wet and miserable on a dirty job involving the heat of the department and the Catholic Church.

She touched his hand and held it.

She drew him to her.

She kissed him and he slipped his hand inside her kimono and touched those places she opened to him. He kissed her breasts and they held each other for a long time.

Rain beat against the panes in the old courtyard apartment building on the Northwest Side, where Karen Kovac lived with her son.

She had a delicate face, with cool, clear skin. Her blond hair was not dyed. She closed her wide, cloudless blue eyes. She opened her mouth and fastened it to his mouth.

They tasted wine on their breaths.

They made love on the couch, which was not comfortable. They made love with hunger. She pressed his large body against her own as though to press it into

39

herself. The rain beat little messages against the windows of the living room and isolated them.

They were not skillful partners but were accustomed to each other by now; they made love like friends. Belly to belly, eyes closed, they only saw the other in their minds, only imagined the pleasure of themselves coming from the other.

And when it was over, Terry Flynn lit another cigarette and sat naked next to her. She did not move to close the robe, which she had not taken from her body. She watched him.

For a long time he stared at the bottle of wine on the coffee table in front of the couch.

"When I was a kid," he began. He paused. "I was an altar boy. I told you that before?"

"No," she said softly.

"I was an altar boy. Me and another kid, it was Tony Galvan, we took a bottle of sacristy wine from the cupboard once before Mass, and after Mass we got pissed drinking it. We went to school buzzed."

"Is that why you failed fourth grade?"

He smiled and took a puff of smoke deep into his lungs. "No. That was something else I haven't got around to telling you yet. You think it's easy being a boy in a Catholic school?"

"No harder than being a girl."

"No," he said. "You never can fake it if you're a boy unless you want to be a wimp. The girls can be sweet and then spread their legs later."

"Like me?" she said, and there was an edge to the banter.

40

He smiled and looked at her. "You're not sweet, Karen. You never were. It's why I like you."

"Is that a compliment?"

"Sure. Take my wife. She was sweet. Tough as nails and sweet. She drove me crazy. I go out one day and there's a kid been trash-compacted by this deranged shine broad because the broad can't stand it that the kid is crying all the time. She's got a trash compactor. She puts the kid in and kills it."

"It."

"It was a her, but it didn't matter when the compactor was done. I never figured out why she had a trash compactor. She lived on Rhodes on the South Side, it was a dump, iron doors, bars on the windows, roaches for breakfast, and she's got a trash compactor."

Neither of them said anything for a moment.

"I come home and she wants to go to the Saint Patrick's Day dance down at the Legion post out in Oak Lawn. I said I couldn't. I didn't even the fuck know it was Saint Patrick's Day. I'm thinking about this mess of goo in a trash compactor and you know what? I can't tell her a thing about it. Sweet girl. It wasn't her fault. She just married the wrong guy."

"Did you try to tell her? Ever?"

"Are you a shrink or what? You know when you can talk to people and you know when you can't. She wasn't a space cadet or anything. She had smarts. But I knew I couldn't never tell her about that. Or anything like that. And it was making me crazy not talking to her. I suppose it was making her crazy, too. It's just as well, I suppose."

"You never talk about your wife."

"Ex-wife," Terry Flynn said. "There's nothing to say to anyone. I don't kiss and tell. Except now I'm sitting here after we screwed, and I'm telling you about me being an altar boy scarfing wine one day because I can't get that priest out of my head. I talked to the little altar boy today, the one who was there, Clarence Washington. He can't get over it. I see it. He's got big eyes and he talks real slow and calm and he can't get over it. One minute you're on the altar and you're thinking these big thoughts about God and you're passing out Communion and the next minute some dude with a .22 slams a couple into the priest and there's blood over everything and you can't get out of it. He scooped up all the Communion wafers. They were in the cup when we got there. Some of them had blood on them."

She squinted because his words hurt her. "Poor Terry Flynn," she said, gently, not mocking, feeling something in herself she could not speak of except in banal terms; it was hidden too deeply in her.

"Not poor me," he said roughly. "Poor sonofabitch when I get him. A fucking cop."

"You don't know that."

"Is the Pope Catholic? I know it. Baby-blue eggshell on his head and he walks in calm and wastes the priest. Who would have the guts for that except us? Some young dope decides to be a priest and does a guy a favor and he ends up with Caffrey at the morgue. Thirty-one years old."

"What favor?"

Flynn paused and considered the stubby butt of his smoldering cigarette and then dashed it out in an ashtray.

"Vacation, I thought I told you. He was filling in at St. Alma's because some other priest was on vacation. Some guy named Father Conklin. Father Bill Conklin."

"Bill Conklin?"

Flynn looked up, surprised. "You know him?"

Her eyes stared through him. "He's a big shot at the University of Chicago. In criminology. I took a course there from him."

"So?"

She bit her lip. It wasn't her business. She and Terry Flynn kept their other lives separate. This was their life together, stolen moments from middle age with the kid at a neighbor's house, screwing like teenagers on the couch in the living room with the rain beating down on the big bay window as background music.

"A bastard," she said at last. "And a phony. I passed the course, but it was a waste of time. He wrote a book; actually, he's written a few of them. He's all over the wall. He doesn't know anything about what he writes about."

"You read his books?"

"One of them. It was *Theory of Justice*. I suppose the 'theory' part means he didn't have to make it have any resemblance to reality." She got up and walked to the small wooden bookcase that also held the television set. She bent down and pulled a book from the shelf and brought it back to the couch. She handed it to Terry Flynn.

Flynn looked at the book and flipped through a few pages and then turned to the back cover. There was a picture of Father William Conklin, professor at the University of Chicago.

"I think I heard of this guy now," Terry Flynn said.

"He was on 'Kup's Show' once or something. Always talking about the Christian virtues of justice and mercy. You're right. He doesn't know shit about anything."

And as he spoke, Terry Flynn stared at the face on the back cover. It was a lean face, somewhat mocking, with penetrating eyes. An Irish sort of face, not extraordinary except for the eyes.

Terry Flynn put the book down on the coffee table. "I thought this guy he was replacing was just an assistant in the parish. We interviewed the priests down at St. Osmond's as well as at St. Alma's and nobody so much as peeps about who this Bill Conklin guy is, so I figured he was just an ordinary mope. Now it turns out he's a writer and a professor. That must be why he had a room at St. Alma's; it was near the university."

Karen Kovac chewed her lip and stared at the face on the back cover of the book.

It really wasn't any of her business, she thought for the second time. But then she realized he didn't see it at all. He might tomorrow or the next day but he didn't see it now.

"Doesn't he look like anyone?"

"Who? This guy? He looks like every priest God ever made. I'm not too crazy about priests, I'm not too crazy about this investigation. Did I tell you the hard time the priest gave my ex-wife when she divorced me? Asshole, I would have . . ."

Terry Flynn stared at the photograph on the back cover. And then he thought he understood. He looked at Karen Kovac. Of course she saw the connection. The story of the murdered priest had been in the papers for a week and all over television.

The same pictures of the dead priest over and over.

An ordinary-looking young man. Typical Irish face. Wavy hair. Not the eyes, of course, but the jawline was similiar.

The two dicks from Area Two had said the old priest at St. Alma's had turned on all the lights in the church after the murder, but for the early Mass, just a few lights were ever turned on. To save electricity.

"Father Conklin was supposed to be saying the seven o'clock Mass," Terry Flynn said dully. "So you think—"

"Not me," Karen Kovac said. "What do you think?"

"The guy was twenty-five feet away, it was raining, the church lights were dim. And all priests look alike when they get dressed up in their robes. But how could it be someone who knew him? I mean, if I saw you across a room, I'd know it was you and not someone else."

"No, that's not true. Say you were upset, thinking about something else, something you had to do. It could be a blonde and she might be wearing the kind of dress I wear, and for a moment you'd think it was me. It happens all the time."

Terry Flynn said nothing for a long moment. He picked up the book again and stared at the face on the back cover.

"And what kind of courses does he teach?"

"Criminology," she said. "A lot of policemen go to his courses. For department credit. The department picks up the tuition for a lot of them."

"What's he like?"

"I told you. A bastard. Arrogant. He doesn't like cops very much."

"A lot of people don't like me but I don't go around killing them," Terry Flynn said. "There has to be more to it than that."

"If that's it," she said. "We're only guessing."

For the first time in a week, Terry Flynn felt like smiling, and he did it now. He turned to her and the smile was so genuine that she had to respond to it.

"Karen does it again. You're better than Matt," he said.

"I hope you don't mean that sexually," she said.

"No, no, you're better sexually, too," he said. And they laughed and he held her suddenly. He felt so much better. It wasn't anything but it was something, as Sid Margolies might say. It was the first break they'd had and Terry Flynn would hang on to it and see if he could pry the break open into a crack.

6
ROGUE COP

At 1:12 in the morning, while Karen Kovac and Terry Flynn slept in her bed in the old courtyard apartment on the Northwest Side, a woman named Charlotta Bray, black, twenty-two, of an address on South Berkeley Avenue on the South Side, turned the corner of Forty-third and Lake Park and started north toward her apartment. There was no one on the street and she felt her familiar panic. She lived in the heart of the South Side black district and knew that any feelings of paranoia she suffered—along with outright fear of attack—were justified.

She walked quickly along the street. She did not use the sidewalk because it was too close to the buildings and too close to the dark gangways that separated the buildings.

When she was ten years old, living in an even darker

heart of the ghetto on Twenty-third Street, she had been attacked by a gang of boys and forced to disrobe and sexually submit to them. The boys had been found later by two policemen who dealt with them with a sort of justice that did not depend on the courts. One of the three boys who had attacked her was found floating facedown in the Chicago River five weeks after the incident; the other two boys were never found. Charlotta Bray had scarcely understood what had happened to her, let alone what had happened to her attackers.

At Forty-second Street, she saw a blue-and-white squad car turn the corner of Ellis Avenue and head east along the deserted street toward her. The squad prowled slowly, as though the occupant was looking for someone or some address.

Charlotta Bray turned the corner and walked along the line of parked cars in the street toward Berkeley, which was one block west of Lake Park Avenue. The squad car pulled abreast of her in the middle of the block between the two streets and stopped. The spotlight on the left-hand side of the hood flashed in her direction. Then the driver's door opened. Charlotta Bray stopped and stared at the policeman who emerged.

"Hey, baby, what you doing out this hour?"

Black man, she thought. "Going home."

"Going home? You been out partying?"

"I been working," she said.

A laugh. She could not see the figure on the other side of the car because the spotlight was in her eyes. She blinked and turned and tried to get the light out of her eyes.

"Working at what? You been tricking?"

"I work at Rayco Can."

"That right?"

"I work night shift. I just coming home."

"Is that right?"

"That's right. I live right over there on Berkeley."

"What address?"

"Forty-one eighty-one," she said.

"Is that right?" The voice was amused but the words came in a monotone.

She started to take a step.

"Hey, baby, get in the car. I'll take you home."

"I ain't getting in no car—"

"Hey, baby, I ain't asking you—"

"I ain't done nothing," she said. "I'm a working woman, I ain't done nothing. Ain't against the law to be out—"

"Baby, I seen you come out of Pap's Tavern ten minutes ago—"

"I—I stopped for a drink. You know. To relax."

"Hey, baby, don't jive me. Get in the car like I say—"

"Oh, man, I ain't done nothing wrong," she said. "I work, I can show you my identity card."

"Okay, baby, just jump into the back there and you show me your ID and I take you home."

She walked around the car in a dream. It was so like a dream that later she would think she had only imagined it. He opened the door to the back seat. There was a cage between the front seat and the back seat. As in all squad cars, the seat smelled of strangers; it was greasy and dirty. She shivered as she bent to slide in.

And then he pushed her. Hard. His hand was on her behind and shoved her across the seat with a slam and she banged her head against the cage.

She knew. She felt sick and there was nothing to do. She pulled at the door handle but the car was locked and the locks were controlled from the driver's seat. It was a car for transporting prisoners.

He was in the back seat next to her. He was hatless. She stared at him, a look of absolute hatred formed in her shining black eyes. And there was nothing to do.

"Now, I know what you do, baby," he said. "And all I want you to do is do for me. You dig that?"

When she was ten years old, two policemen—one white and one black—had sat down with her and her mother in the living room of the apartment on Twenty-third Street and shown them photographs and when she recognized one of the photographs, the two policemen asked her if she was sure and she said yes. They had risen then and said how sorry they were about what had happened and then they went away and she never saw them again. But an uncle who worked as a janitor in another apartment building had gotten the word and he said the policemen had found the boys who had attacked her and he heard the two policemen had killed them. That was what her uncle had heard.

The policeman in the back seat made her do what the boys had made her do when she was ten.

But now she was angry, not confused as she had been then.

And when it was over and she sat away from him, gasping, he said, "Now I'll drive you home."

50

"Just let me out," she said dully.

"All right, any way you want it," he said, and laughed again. Then he turned to the door and pulled at the handle and uttered a long profanity. Stupefied by the attack, Charlotta Bray suddenly realized that her attacker had locked himself into the cage with her and there was no way out.

The policeman then braced himself against her and kicked out at the side window. After three kicks the window cracked, and another kick shattered it. He sat up and brushed away the remaining shards until he could reach his hand out and unlock the door from the outside. He opened the door and surveyed the glass on the street.

"All right," he said at last. "Get the fuck out of the car."

She slid across the greasy seat and stepped on the glass and stood up. It seemed she had been in the car for hours, but it had been less than five minutes. She stared at him for a moment.

"What the fuck you staring at, fucking cunt?"

She turned away then and walked down Forty-second Street to the corner of Berkeley. She walked quickly but calmly. She reached her apartment building and opened the lower door and then walked up three marble steps to the inner door. She unlocked it and entered the foyer. The lights were on. It was a decent building in an indecent neighborhood.

My God, she thought, I feel so dirty.

She climbed the two flights of stairs to her apartment and unlocked the two locks on the steel door and went inside. She dropped her purse on the table in the hall.

Above the table was a crucifix given to her by her mother before she died. Palms from the last Palm Sunday were kept behind the carving of the crucified man.

She went into the living room and picked up the receiver and dialed PO 5-1313, which was the number of the police department. When the bored voice came on the line, she told him exactly what had happened. She had to repeat the story twice. It was automatically recorded by police tapes. The tapes would later become part of the evidence.

7
ADMISSION OF GUILT

Jack Donovan was chief of the Criminal Division of the Cook County State's Attorney's Office. It was the largest prosecution office in the United States, covering Chicago and nearly a hundred suburbs, with a combined population of six million people. On the face of it, Jack Donovan was an important man in the machinery of justice, but Jack Donovan would dispute it. He was a cog, easily replaced when he wore out; he would put it that way. And for the past six months he had felt very replaceable.

The call to his apartment on the North Side came just after dawn. He did not hear the telephone but his daughter, Kathleen, did. She shook him awake with persistence. She was just eleven and very adult because she had to be. She had Jack Donovan to take care of, and no mother to share the burden.

Donovan stumbled sleepily to the telephone in the kitchen. He no longer drank the self-destructive amounts he had consumed when he was separated from his family. But the dull morning feelings persisted, the dryness in his throat, the bleary redness in his eyes. He had once wondered if he were sick. And then he concluded it was merely middle age.

"This is Goldberg," said the perky voice at the other end of the line.

"Why are you so cheerful when you wake me up?" Jack Donovan said. His voice was hoarse but he spoke with something like affection for Goldberg. Goldberg had been too young and eager when he joined he Criminal Division out of law school. Or so Jack Donovan had thought. But in the two and a half years that had passed since then, he had seen that though Goldberg would age, he would never lose that enthusiasm. Jack Donovan had lost it a long time ago, replacing the burden of it with the equal burden of weariness. He was tired of the business of justice because he saw very little that was just in it; he had become cynical in simple self-defense, before his systems overloaded.

"You'll be, too. I know you want in on this from the start. Two Homicide cops from Area Two named Kelly and Hauptmann have put together a nice arrest."

"Stop bubbling over," Jack Donovan said grumpily, and rubbed his hand through his thinning red hair. His eyes were green glass and his face was sallow. The kitchen was too bright for four in the morning, he thought, and he turned off the ceiling light.

"They picked up a call of sexual assault and went over to interview the victim. Black female. Straight. Works at Rayco Can Company on the West Side. Coming home from work, stopped at a tavern on Forty-third named Pap's—"

"Is that still there? Christ, that's been there a hundred years," Jack Donovan said.

"Is that right? She has a couple of drinks and walks home. Alone. And one of Chicago's finest comes by and forces her into the back seat of the squad and makes her give him a blow job."

"You can't prove that—"

"We *can* prove that." Again, the note of triumph in Goldberg's voice. Goldberg did not love policemen.

"Tell me."

"Cop is Ramsey Delford. He's been on the force just over a year, he was sworn two months ago. Part of our recruitment-of-blacks program. Except nobody really checked this guy's record."

"And what is his record?"

"We don't know. Kelly put in a request to the FBI."

"These guys were all supposed to be cleared be-fore—"

"No, Jack, you don't get it." Goldberg was sounding cocky now, but Donovan waited. "They needed black bodies, so when they started doing the record checks, the word came down from the Fifth Floor to forget that crap and get those guys in uniform, so the background check was stopped halfway through. I'm betting this guy was a bad dude—"

"What has this got to do with proof of a blow job?"

"She said he had to kick the back window out to get out after he attacked her because the stupid sonofabitch locked himself in the car. She didn't know who he was, but when Kelly and Hauptmann go by the station to wait for the night shift to come in, this mope comes in with a window kicked out. He said some kids threw a rock through it."

"It happens."

"Kelly says it didn't happen. The window was kicked *out*, not in. So Kelly and Hauptmann talk to the mope and some guys from IID, and after a while our friend allows how he might have done it but she was a whore anyway—"

"He signed a confession?"

"Not yet, but he made verbal admission to six witnesses in Area Two Interrogation."

"Okay," Jack Donovan said in a dull voice. "I suppose I'll come down. The police sheet look good?" Goldberg was in charge of Felony Review, which was the division of the office that checked out police charges at the moment they were filed. The program was funded by the government for reasons of justice. It was used by the politically minded state's attorney to stop hard cases at the source so that the final conviction rate of the office would be high. No one was supposed to take any chances with tough cases unless they absolutely were forced to do so. So said Bud Halligan, the Machine's state's attorney, in a memo to all department heads. It was another reason Jack Donovan felt so tired of the business he was in.

"Letter perfect. Kelly even knows how to touch-type." Goldberg sounded high, his voice sailing with enthusiasm. "But the best part is still coming."

"What?"

"Kelly. He and Hauptmann were originally in on the murder of that priest at St. Alma's last Monday and got bumped when it was shifted over to Special Squad and our good friend Terry Flynn. So Kelly and Hauptmann, when they're talking to the victim, Kelly says he notices this crucifix in the hall of her apartment. She's a nice black girl, shaken up, very straight, neat, you know."

"Does it surprise you that all blacks aren't niggers?" Jack Donovan said.

"Hey, I didn't mean that—"

"Sure you did. You've been hanging around cops too long."

Chastened, Goldberg continued, "He doesn't give it a second thought until he goes after Officer Ramsey Delford and then he thinks about that crucifix. He goes back to the victim, and you know what?"

"She's a Catholic and she belongs to St. Alma's Church," said Jack Donovan. "And that doesn't mean a thing."

Goldberg said, "You're a wet blanket."

"I'm a realist. There are no coincidences."

"Well, Kelly points out that Delford is a policeman and that was a policeman who killed Father what's-his-name."

"His name was Michael Doherty. It was in all the papers."

"Mr. D., we had nine hundred murders last year. I can't remember everyone's name."

"So what does Kelly propose?"

"He would like to clear the priest murder."

"And pin it on Delford?"

"Not pin it on him. He wants to run a lineup and see if the eyewitnesses can pick him out."

"Did he question Delford about St. Alma's?"

"Yes."

"What did Delford say?"

"He said he didn't know what Kelly was talking about. He said Kelly was a turkey sonofabitch who was racist and was trying to pin every fucking crime on the South Side on him just because he was black."

"Was he telling the truth?"

Goldberg paused. "You mean Delford? The sonofabitch just fucked a girl in the mouth in the back of a fucking squad car."

"I know," Jack Donovan said. He could never explain to anyone his reluctance to act. It was so deeply ingrained in his nature that to examine it would require taking himself apart, and he didn't want to do that. It sounded like a good bust. He knew Kelly and Hauptmann. They were rough in the trade because they had been partners out of Area Two for eight years. Justice on the South Side was not the kind of justice people on the near North Side or on the Gold Coast got, but Kelly and Hauptmann were as close to doing the right thing as they could be, under the circumstances.

And Delford was a brother policeman, regardless of his inexperience or the fact that Hauptmann and Kelly were white and that a certain animosity existed in the department between the races. Cops were cops and charging a brother cop was never easy.

"We don't need to do anything today on this priest business," Jack Donovan said at last. "If you've got the charge on Delford on the sex matter, we can hold him awhile. I want to see Kelly and Hauptmann this morning after court. And Terry Flynn, since it's his case now."

"I'll make the arrangement," Goldberg said, with the old eagerness returning to his voice.

"Thanks." Jack Donovan wiped his hand across his lips. "And thanks for letting me know."

"You always told me to call you when we get something like this—"

"Yeah," said Jack Donovan, and he replaced the receiver on the wall telephone. He stared moodily out the window. It was still night. He walked to the window, which was at the back of the flat, and tried to see something in the gloom. A single light illuminated the wooden stairs behind the apartment building and the alley below. Across the alley were garages and, beyond them, small backyards divided by chainlink fences from the other lots and beyond that were the backs of a street of brick bungalows. One light was on across the alley. It was always on this early. He supposed it was a kitchen and the person in the kitchen worked an early shift. It was always on about four in the morning. But, Jack Donovan thought, perhaps the unknown person in the bungalow across the alley was just a mope like himself who awoke before dawn and waited for the morning light because there was no chance to sleep.

Kathleen was standing in the long hall as he started back to his room.

"What is it this time?"

He smiled in the half-darkness at her. My grown-up girl, he thought. She sounded like her mother.

Rita. She had been missing for two years. Everyone had given up on her. She might be dead. She might as well be dead. Poor Kathleen, he thought. Poor Jack. It was what Rita would say to him in the lucid periods of their marriage when he was a cop on Tactical, struggling nights through the courses at DePaul Law School. Poor Jack, she would say, and it would mock his own self-pity.

Poor everybody, he thought, and he gave Kathleen a hug. "Go back to bed," he said.

"What is it?"

"A rape on the South Side." He spoke to her very grown-up because she was. He had begun to realize that children were more grown-up than adults in most cases. "They caught a policeman. He raped her in his car." He did not want to go into the case.

"How could somebody do that?" she said.

"Because people are sick or stupid or tired or drunk or because they don't give a damn," Jack Donovan said.

"A policeman," she said. "It really makes you feel horrible, doesn't it?"

But Jack Donovan realized he felt nothing, not about the policeman, not about the victim. He had long ago decided on the essential sadness of the world and nothing he saw anymore could add one grain of sadness to the burden he already carried.

8
INTERROGATION

Hauptmann put a cup of coffee on the bare wooden table in the interrogation room. The interview room, as it was politely called in official parlance, was white and without windows. The only wall decoration was a chain and manacle for violent prisoners. There were four wooden chairs at the table. Officer Ramsey Delford sat in one of them and stared at the milky coffee in front of him.

"You got anything stronger?" he said in a husky voice.

"You want a drink?" Kelly said. His voice was cold, distant. Kelly stood with his back against one white wall at the far end of the room.

"Something," Delford said in a whisper like gravel.

Hauptmann walked out of the room for a moment. The door closed silently behind him.

"I got to talk to a lawyer."

"You got to talk to us first."

"I know my rights," Delford said. He had said it before in the previous three hours of interrogation. He wondered if it was morning. His face was empty, his eyes red. His blue uniform shirt was partially unbuttoned. His uniform tie lay on the bare wooden table.

"You got no fucking rights, you scumbag," Kelly said. "A fucking policeman. You're a disgrace."

"I know my rights," Delford said.

"No, asshole. You got no rights no more," Kelly said in the same cold voice.

Hauptmann reentered the room. He carried a half-filled bottle of Wild Turkey. He poured a generous shot into the cup of coffee. Delford glanced at him for a moment and then drank, holding the cup with trembling hands.

"Now, you want to talk about the priest?" Hauptmann said gently.

"I know what you guys trying to do to me."

"Fuck, you did it to yourself."

"I didn't do nothing."

"What's nothing, asshole? You put your prick in some woman's mouth and that's nothing? Man, you must be unconscious."

"Look, I'm a policeman, same as you—"

"You dirty motherfucker—" Kelly came off the wall like a halfback off the line and started around the table. Hauptmann pushed himself into Kelly and shoved him back.

"I'll kill that dirty foul-mouthed motherfucker," Kelly yelled.

"Shut up, John, shut the fuck up!" Hauptmann said.

62

John Kelly pulled his piece. "I'm going to kill that scum sonofabitch—"

"John, for Christ's sake, put it away."

"That's a policeman? That's what we got for policemen? I'll kill that scum—"

The door flew open and the two detectives turned in their struggle, partially embraced.

Terry Flynn and Jack Donovan stood framed in the door. No one spoke for a moment.

"He was gonna kill me," Delford said finally.

"Who?" Terry Flynn asked softly.

"That one. Kelly."

"Kelly?" Flynn's voice was almost dreamy. "John, were you going to shoot this man?"

Kelly stared at Terry Flynn for a moment and then placed the pistol back in its holster. He was in shirtsleeves. His tie was askew and his face was unshaven.

"No, Sergeant," John Kelly said.

Terry Flynn stared at Ramsey Delford. "He says no."

"He pulled his fucking piece on me," Ramsey Delford said.

"No, he didn't."

"You turkey cops all the same—"

"Now, Delford. That isn't going to get you anywhere—"

"I want to see a lawyer. I want a lawyer."

"You don't get no lawyer, Delford. I'm ashamed of you," Terry Flynn said. He closed the door behind him softly. He and Jack Donovan stood near the door and stared at Ramsey Delford.

"I got rights."

"You're a policeman, Ramsey. You got no right to wear the uniform and rape girls and kill priests," Terry Flynn said. "But I'll make you a deal. You tell me about it and we'll get you a lawyer. You just tell me about it."

"I got nothing to tell you 'bout nothing."

"Come on, Ramsey. You know the way it plays. You help us, we help you. Isn't that right?"

Delford stared from one face to another. "You doing this to me because I'm black," he said at last.

Terry Flynn smiled. It was not pleasant. "No, Ramsey. If you were black, I'd get you a lawyer and get you charged on the sheet and nobody would say anything to you. But you aren't black. You're a fucking nigger."

Ramsey Delford stared at the face of the Irish policeman across from him.

"You pick up some girl off the street, some girl coming home from work, and you fuck her—"

"I didn't fuck her—"

"You made her suck you off. You put her in a squad and you made her suck you off and then you kicked out the window of your car because you were too fucking stupid to realize you had locked yourself in. You are the scum of the earth, Delford, so what should I call you except a nigger?"

"Why did you kill the priest?" Jack Donovan said.

"I didn't kill no priest, no preacher, no nobody."

"You know what they're going to do with you at Stateville, Ramsey?" Terry Flynn said in a quiet voice. "It's going to take three seconds for everyone in the joint to know you're a cop. Maybe two seconds. Your life isn't going to be worth a pack of Kools, they'll do it for nothing. You want to be hard, you be hard. You want to tell us the truth, you're still a cop, a rotten cop but still a cop. We can take care of you. Move you out of state. You're going to do time but it doesn't have to be in Stateville. You make your plea quiet and we'll keep it quiet."

"Why should I trust you?"

"Because nobody likes this any better than you do. We don't like dirty cops. We don't like cops fucking women on the street and shooting priests. You tell it the right way and you can go salmon fishing in Oregon or whatever the fuck they do in federal joints these days."

Silence. No sound, no clock ticking, not even the sound of breathing for a moment.

"I didn't kill no priest," Ramsey Delford said at last.

"Fine, asshole. I make you a bet you're dead in five days inside."

"Man, you can't do this to me."

"Sure I can. Look. I'm doing it with a smile on my face," Terry Flynn said. "Hell, I'll pay the pack of Kools if it comes down to it."

"You honky motherfucker."

"That's right, nigger."

Jack Donovan did not speak. He stood rigid, too still. He had not interfered; he was not even supposed to be here. He stared at Delford and saw the fear in his eyes. Then he tried to think of images to wipe out the fear he saw, images of the woman named Charlotta Bray raped in the back seat of a squad car. It was no good. He saw only Delford in front of him; he saw only the fear.

He opened the door of the interview room and stepped

out into the subdued atmosphere of the squad room of Area Two. Homicide and Burglary and Auto Theft and the other detective divisions were quartered in glass-walled offices around this large squad room. He blinked in the bright fluorescent light. Morning was red in the sky outside the windows around the room.

He had come from this. He had been a cop once and now he was in a world of such temporizing, such vast areas of gray, of guilt mitigated by other guilts, that he wondered why he had ever left. He was an outsider here, resented by the police as much as by the criminals he prosecuted.

Terry Flynn came out and stood next to him.

Flynn looked at his profile a moment.

Donovan understood the silent question.

"No," Jack Donovan said. "He didn't."

And Terry Flynn couldn't say anything more.

9
WITNESS TO A MURDER

"I want his ass, Ranallo wants his ass, the goddamn Cardinal wants his ass. Not to mention
the man on the Fifth Floor."

As usual, Leland Horowitz was speaking too quickly
and waving his arms about too wildly. He was a small
man past sixty who had once been an agent provocateur
for the Central Intelligence Agency and was now the first
assistant to the state's attorney, Thomas P. "Bud" Halligan. Halligan was a jovial man who hadn't the faintest
idea how the Criminal Division worked. Which is why
his appointment of Jack Donovan to head it was so surprising—Donovan, with his years in the office stretching
back through the terms of several elected state's attorneys,
actually knew what he was doing. But just to make certain
that Donovan never proved an embarrassment, Lee Horowitz, the old Machine fixer and an attorney as well,

was put in day-to-day charge of the divisions under Halligan.

It was Monday morning, a week after the murder of Father Michael Doherty in St. Alma's Roman Catholic Church.

The tall windows of the high-ceilinged office opened onto a light shaft. Somehow it was more depressing than if the office had been windowless. The office was perpetually grimy in summer because of the soot, and in the winter all you could see was the dirt caked on the windows. Now, because of the rain, they were streaked with little aimless rivers that stopped and started and distorted the view. The mood of the office was as gray as the windows.

As always, Jack Donovan half-sat and half-leaned on the ledge of the window on the air shaft. He bent his head and stared at the broken asphalt tile on the floor as he listened to Lee Horowitz harangue him. Jack Donovan had been listening for half an hour. He had not spoken.

"The little black kid, the what's-his-name—"

"Clarence Washington?"

"Washington," Horowitz said. "This kid picked Officer Delford out in the showup. He picks him, Jack. It's a witness, for Christ's sake."

"It's a kid," Jack Donovan said. He closed his eyes and saw Clarence Washington in his mind. The child was afraid from the moment they had brought him into the Area headquarters for the showup. The cops had been indifferent to his fear but Jack Donovan had felt it nonetheless.

Like Kathleen's fear the night Rita had run away. He and Rita had been divorced and Rita had the kids, the boy and girl, and they had lived in Arthur O'Connor's big house in Oak Lawn. Rita had hated their life together, after the kids came, after the warm beginning. He and Rita.

Jack Donovan shook his head, tried to think about the case at hand. But Clarence Washington's big eyes and big fears had inevitably led to thoughts of Kathleen, to Rita. God, we fuck up, don't we?

He and Rita had been friends and lovers since they were children in grammar school. Their marriage was inevitable. Jack Donovan's decision to "go on the department" seemed just as inevitable. It had worked out all right, and then, one afternoon, Jack Donovan realized how sick he was of the business of being a policeman, how impotent he felt in the maws of what passed for the machinery of justice. And when he had spilled it all out to Rita O'Connor Donovan one night as they sat across a kitchen table from each other, she was afraid. Just that suddenly. Just that horribly. It was the first moment of doubt in her life about anything. If Jack wasn't sure, she could never be sure of anything again. And it made her mad. They had two children in twenty-four months and she could not stand the thought of being a mother in a world so uncertain. . . .

"You aren't listening," Lee Horowitz said.

Jack Donovan looked up at the little man sitting behind the large desk that Donovan used to make up his staffing schedules. Lee Horowitz always grabbed the command desk in every room he entered. He even sat behind Bud Halligan's desk when they had conferences in the Civic Center offices of the state's attorney in the Loop. Bud Halligan was envious of the fact that Lee Horowitz, his first assistant, had the largest desk in the SAO.

"Clarence Washington is a kid. He didn't know."

"But you know, right?"

"I was there. I saw the showup. I saw the kid." He paused. "I talked to him. He was scared all the time and he just wanted it to be over with. I talked to his mother. He keeps having the same dream over and over about the priest getting killed, about blood on the Communion wafers. Clarence knew the killer looked like a cop and we had caught a cop and Clarence picked him out of the showup because we all wanted him to pick somebody."

"Jack, you're supposed to prepare the case for the prosecution, not the defense. We pay your salary, not the PD."

"It all comes out of the same pocket."

"They did teach you about the adversarial system of trial at DePaul Law School?"

Jack Donovan let the sarcasm sink of its own weight onto the broken tile floor. He wouldn't pick it up.

"You don't appreciate the situation," Lee Horowitz said. He suddenly stood up and began pacing back and forth like a trial lawyer in front of the jury box. Putting on a show, Jack Donovan thought. He looked down at his hands gripping the ledge of the window he leaned his weight on. The ledge was dirty, the floor was caked with ancient dirt. The windows were always washed by someone, but they were always dirty. Everything in the office was dusty and aged with grime. Donovan's office was one of a series of offices in a rabbit warren strung out along the corridors of the second floor of the old Criminal Courts Building at Twenty-sixth and California. The building was inconvenient to everyone except the prisoners in the sprawling mass of Cook County Jail directly behind the building and connected to it by an underground tunnel. The courts building had been placed in the old neighborhood in the days when it was largely Bohemian by the clout of Anton Cermak, the founder of the Cook County Democratic Machine. As Jack Donovan once observed, the courts were fixed before the first stone was laid.

"I appreciate the situation, Lee," Jack Donovan said at last. He got up from the ledge. "You want to stick out your neck but it's my head that gets chopped off when this indictment doesn't hold up."

"Why isn't it going to hold up? It isn't as if we've got Mr. Clean locked up. Delford is scum."

"That doesn't mean he killed the priest."

"So what?" said Lee Horowitz. "Lock the fucker away for fourteen years. He won't get any more than that, even if the Cardinal himself testifies. And what's he gonna get for the rape? Wouldn't you rather get the rat in court on a decent murder charge?"

Donovan waited a moment because his voice would not have been steady enough. He heard it all the time. He felt the prod from defense attorneys and prosecutors, from crooked judges and deal-making bailiffs. Justice for sale, justice for sale.

"Jack, we go through Delford's apartment, he's a fucking maniac, he's got guns, he's a sex fiend, he has a previous in Detroit for armed robbery. This guy is not *Time*'s Man of the Year."

"He said he didn't kill the priest," Jack Donovan said slowly, patiently. It was the same voice he had tried with Rita for so long, during her hospitalization and after, when she wanted a divorce. The same voice that tried to pick apart the nameless fears for Rita from the fears that were real and had names. It never worked. It didn't work for his son, Brian, who spent days away from home and lived a semi-nomadic existence on the periphery of a crowd that allegedly attended the University of Illinois at Chicago Circle. It didn't really work for his daughter, Kathleen, either.

"I was in the interview room when Delford went around with Terry Flynn. I talked to Clarence Washington. I keep trying to see what motive there is for Delford to do a mad thing like killing this priest during mass. And that's when I figured it out. Delford isn't crazy."

"What's that got to do with it? That's for the defense to plead."

"No. It's for us to figure out before we do the wrong thing. If he raped this woman, it was because he wanted to rape her. There is reason there."

"So he does it in the back of his squad and locks himself in and has to kick the window out."

"I didn't say he was a genius," Jack Donovan said. "I said he wasn't crazy."

"What's that got—"

"He has guns, he's an ex-con, he knows enough to try

to lie his way out of things when he's arrested. What is his motivation in killing the priest? None. None at all. Lee, that's what I'm trying to tell you. The guy who killed the priest."

"Yeah?"

"He's crazy."

"Crazy? You know about crazy people now."

"I know about crazy people," Jack Donovan said in a cold voice and they both understood the reference. "We have shit on this case, Lee. I'm not putting an indictment down on the basis of a nine-year-old eyewitness who couldn't even tell Kelly and Hauptmann at the death scene whether the cop was black or white."

Lee felt himself weakening. He sat down again. "The killer was wearing a police helmet, it was dark in church—"

"So how can Clarence pick him out now in a bright showup room?"

"Jack. I want to level with you."

Jack Donovan tensed. Lee Horowitz never leveled with anyone unless it was the only way to get that person to do something he did not want to do.

"Jack, the Cardinal. He spoke to the Boss this morning."

"Halligan?"

"The Boss, Jack, the man on the Fifth Floor. And the man on Five wants this resolved. He even thinks it is resolved."

"The Cardinal isn't running the Criminal Division, is he, Lee?"

"Look at me, Jack. You know this town. I'm not even a goddamn Catholic. Sorry, Jack."

"It doesn't matter, Lee."

"You know the way it is."

He knew. It was always this way. The clean lines of justice, rights counterbalanced against responsibilities, punishment tempered with mercy—they were ideas for television programs and bar association dinners when the lawyers got together to congratulate themselves. Jack Donovan had given up on being a cop because he had wanted a feeling of power in the system, power to do something right, to make a bigger scratch on life than he made as a cop. He had chosen to go to law school. He had chosen to become a lawyer in the state's attorney's office. And sometimes, like now, he felt as helpless as he had once felt on the streets of the city carrying a gun and wearing the star.

"Lee." Softly. "You're feeling the heat again. Just like we felt it when we had that psycho killing those women last year. You remember that, Lee? We had the wrong man in the shithouse, Lee. You can stand the heat this time a lot better than you can stand another egg on your face."

"Eggs on my face is my business. The Boss called Halligan personally this morning."

"And Halligan genuflected and sent you to do the fix," Jack Donovan said.

"It's my job, Jack. I'm first assistant."

"And I run the Criminal Division."

Pointless. An endless wrangle. Horowitz probed and thrust not because he thought Delford killed the priest in

St. Alma's Church, but because he wanted to see if he could get away with it, take the heat off the office and shove it on some judge or some PD. Someone somewhere else.

"Well, like you say, Jack. It's your head in the noose." Donovan smiled. "And your neck I'm saving."

"The guy is strictly scum, Jack." Sadly. "He isn't worth it."

And Jack Donovan knew it was right. He scratched all day and never made a mark, never made a wrong thing right, never stopped a wrong except by inaction. It was the reason for his perpetual inaction, in fact. He had quit the cops for something that wasn't any better. He had let Rita drift too far away from him to bring her back in. Where was poor mad Rita? She had run away during the investigation of the psycho who killed women; he had taken the boy and girl home with him and they all waited now for the call, from the cops or some hospital or Rita's aged father: They found Rita. They found Rita dead.

"Okay. Don't talk," Lee Horowitz said. He rose and shrugged into his raincoat and looked sadly at Jack.

"I didn't mean about the crazy stuff. Talking about it," he said.

"It's all right."

"You hear anything at all?"

Jack Donovan shook his head.

"The kids. Okay?"

"The kids are okay."

"And the Catholic thing. I'm cocking around, you know. I don't mean nothing about Catholics."

"It doesn't matter, Lee," Jack Donovan said gently.

75

"Okay. Like you said. Maybe I can take the heat. But I hate to do it for a no-good-bum like Delford."

"I know. So do I. But we got him, Lee. I want to keep him tied up awhile. If we declare him the man of the hour, the cops pull off and whoever killed the priest stays out there."

"I'll talk to Bud," said Lee Horowitz of the state's attorney, who rarely came out to the Criminal Courts Building because it was too far from the power of City Hall, from the dining rooms at the Bismarck Hotel where the politicians met and waved pinkie rings at each other daily over lunch.

For a long time after Lee Horowitz left, Jack Donovan sat again on the window ledge and stared at the broken floor. In the gloomy light of the office, he questioned his own conviction about the guilt of Delford. Was it just another excuse to do nothing?

"Mr. Donovan?"

He glanced up and saw Mrs. Keys at the door. She was the ancient secretary who had served five chiefs of the Criminal Division and who would be in the courts long after Jack Donovan was gone. Her longevity gave her a certain sense of superiority over the occupant of the office. The sense carried in the tone of her voice.

"Sergeant Flynn wants to see you?" She made it a question, as though she could scarcely believe Terry Flynn would have made such a request.

Jack Donovan nodded and said nothing. He slid off the window ledge and walked to his desk and perched on the edge of it. He sat everywhere in the office except behind his desk, as though he always wanted to avoid the responsibility inherent in sitting there.

Terry Flynn, wearing his old tan raincoat and a skewed green tie, came into the office clutching a paper cup full of a whitish liquid that might be coffee. He kicked the door shut behind him.

"You got heat yet?" he asked, and both men knew what he was talking about.

"A visit from my friend downtown," said Jack Donovan. "And you?"

"All I know is I wish to fuck that Matt wasn't on vacation in fucking Europe. He was in Miami Beach, I could at least call him."

"What about Delford?" Jack Donovan asked quietly.

"What about him? Another incompetent who also is a fucking rapist."

"How did the police miss that he had a record?"

"Because we were in such a hurry to integrate the department and not lose all that federal money to buy blue Mars lights that we shoved it through on orders from the Fifth Floor," Terry Flynn said.

"He didn't kill that priest," Jack Donovan said.

Terry Flynn paused a moment and sipped the milky liquid in his paper cup. He made a face and threw the remains of the cup in a steel-gray wastebasket near Jack Donovan's desk. He walked over to the battered leather couch and sat down, sinking into the soft old springs.

"I don't think so," he said slowly.

"Why?"

"Because there was no reason for him to kill the priest."

"The girl he attacked was a member of St. Alma's Church."

"Coincidence. You know it the same as I do. Hauptmann and Kelly were the original dicks on the priest murder. When they heard St. Alma's mentioned when they were interrogating Delford, they decided to get smart. They pulled in the altar boy and had a showup and the kid picked Delford. But it's bullshit."

"Is that right? Just happens that way, a cop kills a priest and a week later a cop rapes a member of the parish?"

"Look, Jack, you do what you want. A few hours ago you agreed with me, now I'm agreeing with you. But I don't give a shit for Delford. You want to bust Delford on that one, go ahead, it's your tit, not mine."

"A couple of years ago, you'd be leading the pack," Jack Donovan said.

"Yeah. I got maturity," Terry Flynn said.

The two men stared at each other for a moment. Flynn was beefy and light-haired, with blue, direct eyes and a blunt South Side accent. He had done his time in Vietnam for no other reason than that he was drafted. Some thought he saw life in terms too black and white, us against them; those who thought so were deceived by his manner. An inarticulate subtlety buried beneath the rough words and tough manner made him more than he thought he was; perhaps it was what Karen Kovac perceived in him without understanding her own perception.

"Listen, Jack, I want to clear this even more than you do. Ranallo is on my ass because the superintendent is on his ass and everyone is on the superintendent's ass, from City Hall to the Cardinal's mansion. But I think there's something different going on here."

"What?"

"I was talking to Karen Kovac. You remember Karen."

He remembered. She had nearly been killed the summer before in an attempt to trap a psychopathic killer who had butchered three women. She had been the bait to make him kill again.

"She points out that our victim looks very much like the guy he replaced. Not identical twins or anything—"

"What are you talking about?"

"He was on duty in place of this priest who teaches criminology at U.C."

"Father Bill Conklin," Jack Donovan said.

"You know him?"

"No. And I don't want to. I read some of his crime theories. He had a piece in *Esquire* magazine last spring. He doesn't know anything about it."

"That's what Karen said. She took a course from him once. Lots of cops take courses from him, for credit."

"You?"

"I hate school. I hated school from the first grade. You think I'd actually go to take a stupid fucking course about the kind of shit I'm up to my ass in every day?"

Jack Donovan smiled for the first time that morning and said nothing as Terry Flynn continued.

"The church was dark, it was raining outside, and some cop comes down the aisle and he points at a priest who looks vaguely like Father Conklin and wastes him. You know what I been thinking about over the weekend? I been thinking some cop did what every student wants to do sometime. He killed his teacher."

Jack Donovan got up from his perch on the edge of the desk and walked around it. He stopped and shuffled a piece of paper with another on the desk. Then he looked at Terry Flynn. "Everything is coincidence. You tell me it's coincidental that the woman belonged to this parish and the priest was killed in the parish church. Coincidence. And then the coincidence counts when you give me this theory of Karen's about the two priests looking alike. What does Ranallo say when you tell him that?"

"I don't tell Ranallo dickshit."

"You could make a case for it."

"Look, you don't seem to know nothing about cops."

"I don't? I used to be a cop."

"Then you put on a suit and started talking about habeas corpus. You forget."

Jack Donovan waited.

"They got a rogue cop and he's currently being found guilty in the papers and on television. A bad apple. A black eye for the police department. You know the bullshit routine. The cops only take so much heat at a time. So I'm going to tell Ranallo I got an idea that another cop really did this killing of Father Doherty? Two cops in a week? You think I'm crazy? No. I told Ranallo I was working on a lead about a security guard who might have had a grudge against the Archdiocese."

"Is that true?"

Terry Flynn shrugged. "How should I know? I just

made it up. Ranallo isn't happy but he's got a bone to chew on back in his kennel. And I got Sid Margolies—you remember Sid?—up at the University of Chicago now, checking down a list of students that Father Conklin had. He's looking for someone that maybe Conklin gave an F to."

"That's absurd. You don't kill a teacher because you get an F in class."

"Yeah, tell me. And you don't run a department where you hire on a convicted felon from Detroit just because some pussy federal judge threatens you into it."

"You're not a liberal," Jack Donovan said gently.

"You're fucking right I'm not a liberal. I wouldn't sit in the same squad car with a liberal unless I was arresting him. But that doesn't have anything to do with this. Cops are cops and if they know what the hell they are doing, I don't give a shit if they're black or orange. But I fucking-A am not going to shed tears for a cocksucker like Delford."

"How long can you keep Ranallo off your back?" Jack Donovan asked.

Terry Flynn studied his large hands, which were folded together in the attitude of prayer. "How long can you keep Monsignor Horowitz off yours?"

They studied the problem in silence for a long moment and realized neither of them could solve it.

10
FATHER CONKLIN RETURNS

It didn't work out the way Terry Flynn thought it would. The University of Chicago said the police would have to talk to the professor in charge of a course about releasing grades. Sid Margolies told this to Flynn, who made several remarks that Margolies had expected him to make. Monday passed with a threat of rain and no work done.

Terry Flynn finally reached the residence of Father William Conklin by telephone at 11:00 A.M. Tuesday. The rain had resumed.

He explained about the death of Father Doherty and said he needed to interview the priest and, with unexpected graciousness in his voice, Father Bill Conklin invited him to his apartment. Terry Flynn was about to break the connection when Bill Conklin interrupted.

"You're not going to St. Alma's rectory, are you?"

"That's where you live, isn't it?"

"Hell, no," said Bill Conklin in a voice that seemed an imitation of toughness.

Terry Flynn waited with the receiver wedged between jaw and shoulder. He was busy lighting a cigarette.

"I live at 1200 Lake Shore Drive, apartment 3508," Bill Conklin said. Terry Flynn said nothing for a moment.

"Do you have it?"

"I thought that Father Doherty was replacing you while you were on vacation."

"I'm assigned to St. Alma's but I just can't work there. I have a lot of work to do. I'm working on a new book and there's a piece I'm preparing for *The New Republic*. You just can't work in that neighborhood, let's face it. It's so noisy at night. Shots, sirens, people on the street. I need some quiet, so I rented this apartment about a year ago to get my serious work done. The Archdiocese doesn't like it, of course, but you have to be independent sometimes."

"You can do that? Just not show up for work?"

"This *is* work," Father Conklin said, and his voice was a shade less gracious than it had been a moment before.

"Sure," said Terry Flynn. He replaced the receiver. He stared around him at the cramped room he shared with Margolies and Karen Kovac and Matt Schmidt on the Special Squad. On the wall above the desk that Matt Schmidt used was a calendar from the Federation of Police that boxed off the days into the police department's thirteen reporting units per year. The days of Matt Schmidt's vacation were circled.

"He lives on Lake Shore Drive," Terry Flynn said to Sid Margolies.

"We're talking to him?"

"I'm not sure you're dressed right for it. Don't you have a newer sports jacket?"

"I like this sports coat," said Sid Margolies, hurt by the insult.

"I don't know, Sid," Terry Flynn said. "Maybe you should sit down in the car."

"You don't look so great either. Why do you wear polyester?"

"It doesn't wrinkle," Terry Flynn said.

"It's cheap," Sid Margolies said.

"After we talk to him, we can have lunch over at Kelly's," Terry Flynn said.

"By the El? I didn't know they had lunch."

"Sure. Cheeseburgers."

"Beer."

"That too," Terry Flynn said.

Two hours later they were sitting in an off-white living room in an apartment on the thirty-eighth floor of a high-rise building that commanded a view of the Drake Hotel and the skyscrapers off Michigan Avenue, as well as of the choppy gray waters of Lake Michigan, which lapped to the edge of Lake Shore Drive, below. The apartment was furnished with white couches, white rugs, white chairs, and white side tables. On the walls were photographs that were out of focus. Father William Conklin explained that he was the author of the photographs.

Father William Conklin wore a green Izod shirt and green trousers. His hair was red and the penetrating blue of his eyes was even more startling in person than when viewed on the back cover of a book. Terry Flynn had borrowed the book from Karen Kovac and tried to read it over the weekend. He decided from reading the book that he would not like Bill Conklin very much and he was not disappointed when his feelings were confirmed at the meeting.

"I can't believe that a student would become so incensed over a grade—" Bill Conklin began for the third time, and Terry Flynn's face reddened and Sid Margolies stared out the window at the traffic below.

"Look, Father—"

"Call me Bill."

"Look, Father," Terry Flynn said stubbornly, "I don't know, it's the way I'm thinking, but it might be, and it's worth checking out."

"It's speculation."

"It ain't speculation that there's a dead priest six feet under. That is not speculation. That happened."

"God rest his soul," Bill Conklin said automatically.

Terry Flynn paused to let the prayer sink in and plowed on. "I want to clear this thing as much as anybody. I need your help. I need lists of your students over the past couple of semesters—"

"Quarters," corrected Bill Conklin.

"Whatever. I got to match up who were the cops and who might be security guards and who might have a grudge. I asked you if you knew if anyone had a grudge against you but you can't remember. Maybe you will and when you do, you can call me."

"I can't remember, honestly," Bill Conklin said, like a man who had no enemies in the world simply because he never gave it a thought that anyone wouldn't like him. He sat in a white chair at the side of the couch and sipped a cup of coffee, a beverage that Flynn and Margolies had declined. Against a far wall was a stereo system as well as a neat desk crowned with a beige IBM Selectric typewriter, the only nonwhite item in the room.

"Perhaps you don't understand my position," Bill Conklin said. "Grades are confidential. I like to think that they are a very minor part of the kind of teaching that I do, but nevertheless I regard them as some kind of trust. Perhaps this is not something you care to make the effort to understand, but I feel quite strongly about it."

"I don't want to publish them, I want to get a handle on this thing."

"Don't misunderstand me," Bill Conklin said. "I would like nothing more than to help you with this investigation. I've often written about the crucial nature of the environment for investigation which is created by those people directly affected by a criminal act. But as I've noted, an atmosphere in which such an individual can feel that his input into an investigation is valuable and will be treated with respect must be created over a period of years in which—"

Father Conklin's eyes had become even more penetrating, and he had straightened authoritatively in his chair. A lecture, Margolies thought from his post at the window. Terrific. He's giving Flynn a lecture.

Terry Flynn was angry and it showed in the boiling behind his blue eyes. "This is a case of fucking murder," he said in a barely controlled voice. "Bullets. In the head and in the belly. There is heat on this, coming down from the department and from your church—"

"Flynn? You're a Catholic too, aren't you?"

"Not anymore."

"That's too bad," Bill Conklin said gently, which infuriated Terry Flynn even more.

"No, it's not too bad. My religion has got nothing to do with this or you," Flynn said. He felt lost. He could bully the street people around, he could be rough on the pimps and informers and petty gangsters he had dealt with in the years with Tactical on the South Side. But you couldn't bully a guy who had an eight-hundred-dollar-a-month apartment on the North Side, and white furniture. Frustration made him double his fists; he felt an edge of violence inside himself.

"I want you to help me clear this."

"I can't violate confidentiality."

"Is that like the secrecy of the confessional?" Sid Margolies said suddenly. He had seen an Alfred Hitchcock movie once about a priest accused of murder who wouldn't clear his name because he refused to violate the secrecy of the confessional. It had impressed him at the time as extraordinarily dumb of the priest.

"No, Mr. Margolies, it isn't. But I have some principles."

"Well, Father Conklin," Margolies said calmly because he did not like the man either. "Consider this. If the killer was crazy enough to walk into a church and kill a man in front of four witnesses, and if the killer thought he was killing you, then what makes you think he isn't crazy enough to get the address right this time and finish the job?"

Both detectives watched the very pale, very Irish face.

No emotion for a moment, and then the penetrating blue eyes dulled almost imperceptibly. It was just a moment, like lights dimmed during a power outage. Then Bill Conklin smiled.

"That's an interesting technique of interrogation," Bill Conklin said. "The implication of a threat based on a faulty premise designed to elicit information that is needed for an entirely different premise. A premise I have already indicated that I do not accept."

Terry Flynn gaped at him and then stood up. "Okay. We'll get those grades and we're going to start talking to your students one by one. Instead of going after the ones we can target, we'll talk to every last one of them. Every one. The university can give us a printout of everyone who registered for your courses, including those who dropped out. So we'll just have to do it the hard way."

"Why would you do this to me?" Father Conklin said, and Terry Flynn was startled.

"Do what?"

"Harass me, harass my students?" The voice was mean, bitter, taking an edge that was a mile away from the graciousness on the phone. "This is the kind of harassment I get all the time, you know. From the Archdiocese. Now from you. I know I'm not popular, but I know my theories aren't popular with the so-called street cops. Like you. I know your kind, Mr. Flynn, I've seen them too often. You corrupt the police department with your brutality, your prejudices, your lazy ways of doing things, your utter indifference to the sociological problems of the laboratory you deal in—the streets of Chicago. You don't worry about causes of crime, you don't care about rooting out the sociological perversions at the base of the crime statistics; you're happy to go out and shoot down criminals or beat them up or throw them in jail, where the chances of recidivism rise yearly. Admit it."

"Yeah. I admit it. I like to catch criminals and I do like to beat them up and throw them in jail and I don't give a shit about them one way or another," Terry Flynn said in a cold voice that was charged with the anger that had been building since he entered the apartment.

"This is official harassment and I won't have it."

"Well, you got it anyway, Jack," said Terry Flynn in the rough street argot of his native South Side. "I got a dead man and I got heat and I'm going to clear this thing one way or the other. I wouldn't care if the victim was a whore in a three-stool blind pig; he's my victim and now I got to avenge him and that's the way it works. I read your book, it stinks." Sid held up a hand but Terry Flynn ignored him. "You don't know shit about what you're talking about."

The priest smiled then, which was as unexpected as the bitter tone of a moment before. "But I know about policemen and I know about crime and I know your category in the whole rat race. You're a limited, low-level functionary in a bureaucracy that hasn't essentially changed in a hundred years."

"And you're a priest, which saves you from having me beat the living shit out of you—"

"I thought you weren't a Catholic, Detective Flynn."

Terry Flynn stared at the man in the white chair with undisguised contempt. "I still got religion," he said finally, and it was the last thing said among the three of them.

11
I DON'T CARE WHO YOU ARE

What happened on Tuesday night, eight hours after the bitter interview between the two homicide detectives and an arrogant priest named Father William Conklin, was the kind of random act that always seems to complicate a major murder investigation.

The Archbishop of Chicago alighted from his black Lincoln limousine at 9:45 P.M. in front of Holy Name Cathedral and considered for a moment what he had wrought.

The cathedral was a century old, built of soft Illinois limestone that had softened further over the one hundred years until the great steeple in front of the church was in danger of crashing over in a high wind and scattering stones all over the seamy near North Side edge of State Street. By dint of will, the "builder priest," as the Cardinal had been called forty years before in his first parish, had raised nearly two million dollars to restore the crumbling cathedral to its former magnificence. The fact that the cathedral was essentially a homely prairie structure, built for the years and not for the ages, did not dim his zeal. The millions were spent shoring up the crumbling foundation laid haphazardly in the soft, marshy Chicago soil of 1873, and in restoring the appointments inside the church. Two massive wooden doors that, despite their weight, opened with the slightest touch, had been dedicated the previous December.

The Cardinal Archbishop of Chicago saw what he had done to the cathedral and it was good; the thought of his heroic labors never bored him. He knew he was not an intellectual, nor even particularly popular among the three million Catholics in his archdiocese; but he had used his grasp of Church politics to a good purpose.

Which is why he would drop by the cathedral from time to time, always alone, without his robes of office, dressed as a simple rotund priest who came to the church he had so lovingly restored, to pray to God to forgive his many sins.

As always, the limousine prowled quietly around the corner of Chicago Avenue to park discreetly in a no-parking zone at the side of the cathedral, where the driver unfurled his copy of the *Daily News* and waited for his Archbishop to finish his private prayers in the church.

And that is why the limousine driver, Alfredo Gatazzi, did not see the young black man approach the rotund priest on the steps of the cathedral and did not know the full story of what transpired, even after the incident. It might have been embarrassing to the Archbishop of Chicago to reveal all the conversation.

The young black man, dressed simply in a black shirt, brown jacket, and jeans, and wearing tennis shoes, had produced a small pistol—probably a .22 Special, as the police called the trash guns—and said: "Gimme your wallet, preacher."

The Archbishop of Chicago, who had never been robbed, did not know what to say and so he said something: "I'm the Cardinal."

And the young man replied—it was all ludicrously recorded in the police record of the incident—"I don't care if you a turkey buzzard, you gimme your motherfucking wallet or you ain't gonna whistle no more."

And so the Archbishop of Chicago was robbed of thirty-eight dollars, a leather wallet, and a large diamond ring. He was not hurt and the young robber was gone into the shadows of Superior Street within seconds. He was never caught.

MORE VIOLENCE AGAINST THE CHURCH. The provocative headline was to be expected in the editions of *Chicago Today*, but it accurately recorded a public mood.

By now, Terry Flynn felt punch-drunk from the daily battering by Commander Leonard Ranallo of Homicide and the man from the superintendent's office, but he plowed on. He and Sid Margolies had spent two straight days going through police personnel records and trying to match them with class records provided by the registrar's office at the University of Chicago.

It was nearly midnight on the day after the Archbishop was robbed when they finished. They were sitting in the cramped little office provided for the Special Squad on the seventh floor of police headquarters. On their desks were paper cups half-filled with milky coffee and littered with the remains of half-smoked cigarettes. Half-empty cartons of Chinese food also testified to the numbing task the two detectives had set themselves.

"My butt feels like it's asleep," Sid Margolies said with some concern.

"If you can feel it, it can't be numb," Terry Flynn said in a hoarse voice caused by too many cigarettes and not enough beer. "I think we're finished. It's hard to believe so many cops go to listen to that fruitcake."

"We're finished and what do we got?"

"I see five names. Do you see five names?"

"I think so. It's hard to say. My eyes feel numb, too."

"You want to run down their assignments on the day Father Doherty was killed?"

"No. I want to go home and have a nice session vomiting in my own toilet." Margolies's face was ashen; in fact, he had thrown up in the lavatory down the brightly lit hall from the office.

"You didn't like the food?" Terry Flynn said wearily, just to say something, just to keep awake. His eyes were red-rimmed and his face was stubbly with reddish beard.

"No," Sid Margolies said seriously. "It was terrible. I like Chinese food but this wasn't Chinese food."

"The hell it wasn't. The guy was Chinese, wasn't he?"

"He wore a rubber band across his eyes to make them

look slanted," Sid Margolies said. And he did a rare thing that he could never have imagined himself doing: he giggled.

"Go home, Sid," Terry Flynn said after Sid had stopped giggling.

"You going home?"

"I'm going to run down where these guys were supposed to be working on the day."

"Who elected you Iron Man Bronsky? I'm tired. Aren't you tired?"

"I'm thirsty," Terry Flynn said. "If I get through this in an hour, I still got time to get up to Kelly's for a six-pack and two cold ones in the bar. Then I'll be tired. I'll sleep then."

"I'll stick around," Sid said.

"Go home, Sid. What are you gonna do, hold my hand while I look up their assignments?"

"Yes, I like blondes. Did I ever tell you that?"

Exactly fifty-one minutes later, they had checked all five names of potential suspects against their assignments on the day Father Michael Doherty was killed at Mass. Three were on days off and two were assigned to districts on the North Side.

"We can't do any more tonight," Terry Flynn said. "First thing in the morning, we talk to the three guys who were off that day and we check out the districts of the other two guys to see where they were clocked around seven in the morning."

"Okay, I'm going home. You got a car?"

"No. I'll jump on the El and—"

"I'll give you ride," Sid said. They walked out of police

headquarters and blinked as though surprised to find that the city still existed. They had been inside the building for twelve hours. Flynn had even sent out for the Chinese food rather than interrupt the checklist.

Sid Margolies found a parking ticket on his windshield. He pulled it from beneath the windshield wiper and stared at it.

"We serve and protect," he said slowly, repeating the department motto painted on the doors of the blue-and-whites. "And some silly bastard with nothing better to do gives me a ticket."

"You were parked in a no-parking zone," Terry Flynn said.

"So what? I'm a policeman. I'm supposed to get away with parking in a no-parking zone. Shit." He opened the car and climbed inside. Terry Flynn slid into the seat next to him.

For a moment they sat in the car without speaking. The weather had turned cooler but it had not rained for two days. The sky was red from the city lights painted against the clouds.

Sid Margolies opened his glove compartment and removed a stack of parking tickets bound with a rubber band. He added the newest ticket to the top of the stack and replaced it.

"You're a fucking scofflaw," Terry Flynn said dully. "It's my sworn duty to arrest your ass. I think I'm going to shoot you."

"Go ahead. I can take it." Silence. "Terry, they're going to push Delford into it, aren't they?"

"Tomorrow. I talked to Jack Donovan. It's getting out

of control. Delford looks like a setup except they can't seem to figure out any motive to pin it on him. They'd like to clear this one. Just to get the Archdiocese off their back. Jack said the Cardinal was hysterical. Jack said he got a visit from the Fifth Floor."

"Not from Himself?"

"When God wants something done, He sends out Gabriel, doesn't he? No, the Mayor's fixer came by and Jack talked to him a long time and tried to make him see that just because the heat is on, you can't start pinning shit on every mope you got locked in County Jail."

"Why not?"

Terry Flynn blinked. He looked at his watch. "It's five after one. I got fifty-five minutes to get to Kelly's. You think you can get up there in ten?"

"I'm a policeman, right?" Sid Margolies said.

They made it in nine minutes using the horn and the siren.

An emergency run of sorts.

12
BLESS ME, FATHER

His mind wandered as the old woman recited her sins.

Father Bill Conklin was administering the sacrament of Penance, which Catholics informally called "confession." He sat in a small, boxlike closet of a room, in the dark; as with most confessional chambers, on either side of this central closet was another where confessors came, knelt in darkness, and spoke their sins to him. He had two sliding screened "windows" of wood that alternately sealed one confessional chamber while a penitent in the other was reciting his sins and his prayers. It was just after four on a Saturday afternoon twelve days after the murder of Michael Doherty in this very church. He was listening to confessions.

Normally he would not have been here, but the death of Michael Doherty had upset him and he felt some penitential need to perform routine parish duties. At least for a while.

Father Hogan, the old pastor, was not a friend, but the old man had urged Father Conklin not to go to the church. "Maybe that killer is still there, waiting for another priest," the old man had said.

Father Conklin had offered him a faintly superior smile. His intense blue eyes gleamed, as though preparing for combat.

"You go there every day."

"Because I have to. You don't have to," the old priest said. He still wore an old-fashioned cassock with buttons from toe to collar. He had white parchment skin, dry and wrinkled, and his hands were slightly palsied. If the need of St. Alma's Church for a priest—any priest—had not been so great—at least in the thoughts of Father Hogan—he would have been long retired.

"Father, I think I need to do this," Father Conklin had said.

The old man had smiled without pleasure. "Are you feeling guilty about Father Doherty's death?"

"There but for the grace of God go I," Conklin had said pompously.

"So you've come down for a few days to work as an ordinary priest, sort of like a retreat," Father Hogan had needled him, not so gently.

Father Conklin had stiffened. "If you'd rather I went—"

"Now don't get snooty on me, son," Father Hogan had said. "Whatever your motives, I can use the help. Go on over to the church this afternoon and take on the confessions. I've got to go see Ed Collins about the roof. We can't take another winter with the roof in that condition. The water is running right down the walls now, as it is. We get a lot of snow, and next spring the church will look like an indoor swimming pool."

And so Father Conklin was in his final half hour of hearing confessions and dispensing the sacrament of Penance.

The old woman had finished her mundane catalogue of errors and Father Conklin raised his right hand in blessing. "For your penance, say five Our Fathers and five Hail Marys and now make an Act of Contrition."

"O my God, I am heartily sorry for having offended Thee. And I detest all my sins because I dread the loss of heaven and the pains of hell. But most of all . . ."

She rattled off the ritual words and Father Conklin mumbled the blessing and then it was over and he slammed shut the small wooden panel over the screen. Because both he and the penitent were shrouded in darkness, and because of the wooden screen, he could not clearly see the penitent and the penitent could not clearly see the priest.

He uncovered the opposite window by sliding the small wooden panel along the track. A figure knelt at the screened window; the figure was quite large.

For a moment there was silence.

Nothing but the sound of breathing.

Conklin felt suddenly frozen in his chair. My God, my God, it's happening to me, he thought, just the way it happened to Mike Doherty. But it couldn't happen to me.

I have my books, my career, I serve the Lord in a different way, I want to be a good priest, I really do, I—

The panicked thoughts were broken by the voice from the other side of the screen.

"I want to tell you something."

Another long moment of silence lay between them.

"You. Want to make a confession?"

"I want to tell you something."

Conklin said nothing.

"I killed that priest," said the whispery voice.

Father Conklin felt entombed in the box of the confessional. He had locked himself in—a precaution suggested by Father Hogan because of the odd nature of the neighborhood and the sort of people who wandered into a church to rob the priest—and it would take too long to unbolt the confessional door. Does he have a gun? Does he have it pointed at me right now?

"Are you listening to me?" the whisper demanded.

"I'm listening to you," Father Conklin said, and he thought his voice sounded suddenly small.

"I killed the priest."

Silence.

In the dark box, Father Conklin felt sweat pressing against his clothes. Sweat beaded on his forehead. His blue eyes were shining as though with tears. His nostrils were wide and flaring as adrenaline pumped through his body.

"Do you know why?"

"My God, man—"

"I thought he was you."

Conklin realized his heart was beating too loudly. His hands pressed against the sides of his wooden chair, as though trying to drive flesh through the wood by force of will. He was absolutely still.

The whisper continued, but the shadowy outline of the large head did not move. "I got to tell you this so you understand."

"Why would you want to kill me?"

"You know why."

"I don't even know you."

"You know me," the whisper said.

"I don't, I don't."

"It doesn't matter. I don't want to kill you now. I can't get that priest out of my head. I keep seeing him pitch over, I keep seeing that little altar boy turned around to look at me. I can't get none of it out of my head. I never killed anyone in my life. My God, I must have been crazy, I hated you so fucking much. I was half stiff, I just came into the church and I didn't know what I was going to do, I just thought maybe I'd wait around for you or something. I sat in the back of church for a while and I kept thinking about you and I got crazy or something. I been drinking. I was drinking too much. I wouldn't have done it if I hadn't been drinking, I don't think. I don't know what I had in mind. I came up when the people were coming up and he sees me and comes down to me, only I still thought it was you, I been up all day and night, he looked like you, all you priests look the same, and I had the gun out and you know what?"

"What?"

101

"I had the gun out and I knew I'd have to use it then. I didn't even think about it until I saw it in my hand and then I didn't think about it for a second and then I let you have it. Pow. Pow." The whisper imitated the soft whooshing sound of a pistol fired in a closed room. "It was loud. I never even shot a gun once, except on the pistol range. Not once. And then that little boy looks at me, all scared, and I came to my senses."

Conklin waited. His hands had not moved. His face was wet with perspiration. The man who said he was a killer continued to whisper. He rambled on and on, explaining himself, explaining why he had come to kill Conklin that Monday morning. Conklin sat still, answering perfunctorily as sweat trickled down his forehead and burned his eyes.

"I didn't mean to kill him," the whisper finally said, and then it broke suddenly in a sob. "I was so mad, I was crazy. I got to tell you that. I was crazy. You made me crazy."

"You should tell the authorities and—"

"And what? They'll put me in the shithouse for the rest of my life. Are you crazy?" The whisper sounded surprised by the suggestion. "I want God to know what I did was wrong and I know it was wrong and I'm gonna make it up to Him."

"What do you want from me?"

"I want you to bless me."

"But I can't ask God to forgive you when—"

"I want you to bless me," the whisper said in a strange, distant way.

Slowly, Father Conklin raised his hand. He saw that it shook, just as the hands of palsied Father Mike Hogan shook.

He began to make the Sign of the Cross in the darkened air.

"Say the words," said the whisper.

"God bless you in the name of the Father and of the Son and of the Holy Spirit."

And God forgive me, Bill Conklin thought as he finished the blessing of the murderer.

13
GLOOMY MONDAY

It was a strange Monday, disjointed and dreamlike; they all would remember that later. It was as though events were taking place that had been lifted out of reality but remained vaguely associated with it.

It began with the presentations to the Cook County Grand Jury on the evidence against Patrolman Delford. The members of the jury, some bored and some uncomfortable, were led through the presentation by Mario DeVito, one of the old-time prosecutors left in the office.

A grand jury is established in law as an independent body of citizens with broad powers to consider evidence and decide whether there is enough evidence to permit a public trial. In truth, however, a grand jury, with rare exceptions, is happy and relieved to follow the prosecutors' lead; twenty-three strangers pulled out of their everyday occupations and plunged willy-nilly into the intricacies of the criminal-justice system have little choice.

Or, as Lee Horowitz put it that morning to Jack Donovan: "I want that fucking jury to throw a ton of bricks and bury that black cocksucker and I want it by noon."

Donovan reluctantly agreed to present the circumstantial evidence against Patrolman Delford in the murder of Father Michael Doherty, as well as the shaky evidence of a single eyewitness, a terrified nine-year-old altar boy who had caught a bare glimpse of the killer. Delford, who was free on bond, had true bills reported by the grand jury accusing him of murder, sexual attack, and criminal destruction of city property (in the matter of a broken window in his squad car).

A court-approved search of Patrolman Delford's property had uncovered nothing directly linking him to the murder of Father Doherty. But the police detectives assigned to the case had uncovered a cache of weapons that would have won approval from a terrorist cell: four shotguns, one M-16 semiautomatic rifle, six pistols (including three .22-caliber pistols that were test-fired to see if the slugs matched those that had killed the priest) and a variety of exotic weaponry, including a Japanese samurai sword set.

The separate true bills were signed at 11:45 A.M. by Judge Harry O'Neal in his office behind the courtroom on the sixth floor, thus changing them into indictments. The indictments were turned over to the police by 12:10 P.M., and Patrolman Delford, suspended from his duties until the outcome of the trial, was arrested at home by 2:00 P.M. In the matter of murder, said Judge O'Neal, there would be no bail.

About the time the Cook County grand jury was returning its true bills against the policeman, Terry Flynn walked into the little cramped office shared by the members of the Special Squad on the sixth floor of the police headquarters building at 1121 South State Street.

It had been a fruitless weekend. None of the policemen whose previous records in the department and whose attendance at a class given by Father William Conklin might have indicated an inclination to violence had panned out.

Three of the five policemen were on the North Side in far distant districts that day, and all had been registered on call-ins to account for the time of the murder of Michael Doherty.

One of the policemen was in Presbyterian–St. Luke's hospital with cirrhosis of the liver.

The final policeman had been on leave during the day of the murder. It turned out he had been on a family reunion picnic in Eagle River, Wisconsin; this was attested to by several members of the family. Eagle River was nearly four hundred miles north of Chicago.

"That gives us Delford," Sid Margolies had said glumly. He didn't like the business any more than Terry Flynn did. It was not a matter of police loyalty to another policeman in trouble. Neither Flynn nor Margolies nor anyone else in the case had expressed sympathy for Delford. They all thought he was a rapist and had used his police power, his authority to arrest, to commit a crime.

"I don't give a shit who it gives us. It's the wrong guy," Terry Flynn said.

"Well, there's nothing we can do about it," Sid Margolies said. And it was perfectly true. There was nothing any of them could do about it. The machinery of justice—the real machinery, not the engine described in civics lessons—had its own peculiar momentum. When there was a rush to judgment, it was best to stand out of the way.

In this downhearted mood, Terry Flynn expected nothing when he walked down the long corridor on the sixth floor and into the office. He forgot it was the day Matthew Schmidt was returning to duty.

Matt Schmidt had twenty-eight years in service. He was a calm man who always seemed to wear the same attire: a blue suit and a hat and a white Arrow shirt with a starched collar and a narrow, dark-hued tie of no particular pattern. He also wore the manner of a man who did not expect much from life but did not worry unduly about it. His manner was earned; he had beaten lung cancer four years before. At least he hoped he had. As in other things, he had taught himself not to worry more than necessary about survival. He was a lean, cadaverous man with pale skin and brooding eyes and a certain sternness to his jawline that invited respect. He had bearing and presence without trying to have these qualities; perhaps it was the only way they were obtainable.

Now Lieutenant Matthew Schmidt turned slowly in the creaky swivel chair with the wooden back. His right hand remained on his desk, still clutching a report on the murder of Father Doherty two weeks before.

"Christ, I'm glad to see you," Terry Flynn said, putting down his paper cup full of pale coffee. He extended his hand.

"No welcome back?"

"I said I was glad to see you," Terry Flynn said, shaking hands.

"But that isn't the same thing," Matt Schmidt said, and Terry Flynn smiled.

About the time the *Chicago Daily News*'s criminal-courts reporter was phoning in his highly colored account of the crimes with which Patrolman Delford was charged in the indictments, Terry Flynn was telling the story of the murder of a priest and of the rape to Matt Schmidt. He told it as a child or as an eager student, certain the listener would be able to see clearly what he could not see and solve the problem.

"Delford didn't kill the priest?" Schmidt finally said in a gentle voice. He was a gentle man, a soft cloak of politeness and courtesy thrown over the iron that was his core.

"No," Terry Flynn said.

Schmidt smiled. "I always get a straight answer from you, at least."

"I wouldn't mind if they cut the creep's balls off and stuffed them in his mouth. But he didn't kill the priest, which means someone killed the priest and he's still out there."

"How does Father Conklin strike you?"

Terry Flynn lit a Lucky Strike. "He strikes me like a bowl of shit for breakfast."

"Graphic."

"He's an asshole. No cooperation. But we can't lean on him. He's not only a fucking priest but a professor at the University of Chicago. The liberals would love to skin us alive and the Catholics would roast us in hell."

"Maybe we should talk to him again," Matt Schmidt said.

"I want you to do that," Terry Flynn agreed. "I don't have any tact with these guys."

"Maybe I won't either."

"You, Matt? You'll have him eating out of your hand. I wanted you to come back. I knew you must have come in over the weekend, I was going to call you, but then I figured Gert would give me hell, and besides, you must have had jet lag."

"I'm a little tired," Matt admitted.

"Nice trip? How was Europe? Still full of foreigners?"

"Very nice," Schmidt said in a gentle voice.

"Happy to be home."

"No," Matt Schmidt said. "I could drift away forever."

"Take me along," Flynn said.

"I'll adopt you."

The next dream in this moody, dreamlike day came at two in the afternoon, when Father William Conklin escorted the two policemen into his white-on-white apartment on the thirty-eighth floor of the building on Lake Shore Drive at the very moment Delford was being arrested in his apartment. Sid Margolies was not present. Father Conklin had replaced his facile charm with polite civility. He took both of them to the same room where Terry Flynn had first confronted him. Again, Terry Flynn felt uncomfortable with the white furnishings and white rug, the slightly decadent sense of propriety that perfumed the air of the room.

"Lieutenant Schmidt," Father Conklin said stiffly. "I've already spoken to your colleagues."

"Yes," Schmidt said. "Do you mind if I sit down?"

"Not at all. I didn't know you were connected with this case."

"I wasn't. I was on leave. I'm just back and I wanted to talk to you about the death of Father Doherty."

"Vacation?"

"Yes."

"Where?"

Matt Schmidt made a little face and then thought better of it. "Europe. Germany, mostly."

"I love Europe," the priest said. "Can I get you something? I've just purchased some very nice, unpretentious Chablis. California, I'm afraid."

"No, thank you," Schmidt said. "I want to take as little of your time as possible, Father. You may have a clue in your records to the man who killed Father Doherty." The abruptness of Lieutenant Schmidt's speech altered the atmosphere in the room again; now the condescension of the priest was replaced by an air of aggressiveness.

"That's what Sergeant Flynn said. I appreciate your position." For the first time the priest lowered his eyes, as though considering something else. "You have to understand my position."

"No," Matt Schmidt said. "I do not."

The priest seemed startled out of his reverie. He stared at the man in the plain blue suit and white shirt and plain tie. The eyes of the older man stared back, not in threat

110

and not for effect; they were calm, lazy eyes that seemed to miss nothing.

"This is a murder investigation," Matt Schmidt said slowly. "Are you obstructing it?"

Conklin was pale but he smiled now and his penetrating blue eyes seemed to sparkle. "I'm aware of the law. No one has mentioned obstruction of justice before. As I said, I know the law. After all, I teach the subject."

"Then you should be aware of the position you've put us in. The position you may have put yourself in," Matt Schmidt said in the same deliberate voice. Terry Flynn sat opposite the two men and watched the confrontation with the same absorption he would give to watching a prize-fight.

"We need your information to find the man who killed Father Doherty," Matt Schmidt said. "You withhold it. That is obstruction."

"Then arrest me," the priest said.

"It could come to that," Matt Schmidt said.

"Oh, Lieutenant. Don't be tedious. You're not going to arrest me, because you already have your murderer. I heard it on the radio this morning. One of your own policemen."

"The investigation is not over," Lieutenant Schmidt said stubbornly. "Was Officer Delford ever in one of your classes? Did you know him for some reason?"

"I never laid eyes on him."

"Then why would he want to kill you?"

The priest blinked and said nothing for a moment. "What do you mean?"

"The man who killed Father Doherty thought he was killing you."

"That's what Sergeant Flynn said." Father Conklin blinked again, and this time Flynn thought the priest's perpetually pale color had whitened even more. "I don't accept that theory."

"There was no reason to kill Father Doherty," Terry Flynn said.

"But there is reason to kill me. Is that it?"

"Perhaps," Terry Flynn said.

"What if it was merely an act of passion, carried out by someone with a grievance—real or imagined—against the Church or against priests in general? Or even, accepting your theory, against me? What does it matter now. Poor Father Doherty is dead. It is over." The priest got up suddenly and began to pace the room, staring down through the windows at Lake Shore Drive below. "Justice is based on punishment, but you and I both know that justice, even when it works in our system, is faulty. A few months ago a career burglar was convicted of stealing a television set belonging to the daughter of a close friend of the mayor. He got sixteen years in prison. Admittedly, he was a careerist in crime, but was it just to administer a sentence of sixteen years for an act so petty?"

"We don't sentence criminals. We catch them," Terry Flynn said.

The priest turned from the window. He was smiling. "That's absurd and you know it. You hardly ever catch anybody, according to your own statistics. You solve murders because they are solved for you—the murderer stands around with the smoking gun in hand or it is obvious that a husband has killed his wife or vice versa. But how many crimes of murder do you solve using detective work, insight, logic? Very few."

"More than you'd think," Terry Flynn said.

"Take the case of Father Michael Doherty. A man dressed as a policeman walks into a church one morning and kills him and walks out. The story is on the front page day after day. All the powers of the police are brought to bear; there is a hue and cry. But what is at the core of this massive show of force on the part of the police department? The core is empty. You have nothing but dull instincts. You demand to see my private records on my students because one of you has a hunch that the killer intended to murder me, not Michael Doherty. But what do you know about Doherty? Did he have a secret enemy in his past who suddenly surfaced at that time and place and killed him? Was he merely the innocent bystander to a traffic accident that happens to involve him as well? Who can tell? But if the human brain is capable of pursuing many thoughts almost instantaneously, the police cannot do so.

"They fix on one thought at one time and worry it to death. The theory is that I was the intended victim. But why? What have I possibly done in my life to so enrage an individual that he would risk his life to take mine?"

"We don't know," Matt Schmidt said calmly, breaking the monologue. "That's what we would like to find out."

"Listen. I am a priest. At the same time, I am a writer, a practicing intellectual, a theorist, a professor at one of the great institutions of learning in this country. Do I say these things too proudly for you? My life is complicated, is what I'm trying to say. I could sit here with you for days and talk about acquaintances and friends and friendly enemies and academic pals and it would give you enough material to pursue this case for ten years. But in the end, would any of the leads be accurate? Do you see what I'm saying?"

Terry Flynn did not, but he said nothing.

Matt Schmidt stared at the priest for a moment before speaking. "I'm not talking about your past life, Father. This man killed two weeks ago. Something built up in him quickly."

"Rage?"

"Perhaps. But whatever it was, he did a mad act. He probably didn't even intend to kill you or the person he thought was you. Maybe he was drunk or on dope. He walked into a church in uniform and walked right up where four people could see him and shot Michael Doherty." Schmidt paused for a moment, reconstructing the act of murder in his mind's eye. "We think he shot the wrong man. He meant to shoot you. Will he try to make amends for his mistake by killing the right man? I don't know. Do you want to gamble with that? It's your life."

"Why do you insist the killer meant to kill me?"

"Because you should have been in that church on that morning saying Mass," Matthew Schmidt said. "You were not there. You and the dead priest bear some slight resemblance to each other. The church was poorly lit. It was raining and it was dark outside. The back lights of the church were never turned on for the early Mass because there were so few people attending it. Given all these indications, why isn't it reasonable to assume there is a motive to the murder instead of no motive at all?"

"You have remarkable insight, Lieutenant," Father Conklin said with a grudging smile. "I think your theory about the killer is correct. I don't think he intended to kill me. I think he didn't know what he intended right up to the last moment. Let's say the theory is correct."

Schmidt waited.

"If it is correct, then why pursue the matter any further? Punishment comes, whether it comes from the state or from God. He's suffering now, he has remorse, it's hurting him every moment he's awake to think of what he's done."

"I'm not concerned with theology," Schmidt said. "I'm concerned with the punishment of the here and now. The man stepped outside society when he committed murder, and society is going to do what it has to do to catch him."

The priest said, "You don't catch everyone you go after."

"We try," Matt Schmidt said.

"Nonsense. There hasn't been a syndicate murder ever solved in this city, and how many have there been? A thousand over the years? You don't try, not equally, and—"

Terry Flynn spoke for the first time. He had been lost in a sort of soft concentration on something he had just heard. It had not been the words as much as the tone of voice. Yes, he had decided—it was the tone of voice, it had been too certain.

"You seem to know a lot about the murderer," Terry Flynn said.

Both the priest and the lieutenant stared at Flynn, but Flynn was looking only at the priest. His blue eyes were marble-hard and his manner was unyielding. He wasn't in an expensive apartment on Lake Shore Drive anymore; he was on the street with a punk against the squad car hood, asking questions that pricked the skin.

"You said he was feeling remorse, he didn't want to kill anyone—"

"Sergeant, I was speaking theoretically—"

"No, you weren't. Not at all. You know the sonofabitch."

The priest stared back at the sergeant and neither man spoke.

"You know who the sonofabitch is," Sergeant Flynn said.

"No." Hesitantly. "Not really—"

"It wasn't Delford."

"No. I honestly don't think so."

"You honestly don't think so?" Lieutenant Schmidt said sharply. "What does that mean?"

"I don't know who the killer is, I can assure you—"

"I can assure you that you know a helluva lot more than you've been telling us," Flynn said. "I'm tired of these games with you, Father. I'm tired of your goddamn theories of crime." Flynn got up and walked to the window. On a table by the window was a small glass angel made of Waterford crystal.

Terry Flynn picked it up and looked at it for a moment,

and the priest and the lieutenant stared at him and said nothing.

Terry Flynn dropped the angel on the table and it shattered. Halo was broken and wings were reduced to shards.

"Look—" began Father Bill Conklin, rage and the edge of fear struggling on his features. He stood up.

Flynn turned. "No, you look. You've got a couple of lives hanging on your conscience—that is, if your ego lets you have a conscience anymore. One is Delford. Delford may be a lowlife asshole but he didn't kill anyone and you know it but he went to bat this morning and now he's in County Jail with a heavy indictment pinning him down. Two, you got the life of the real killer who is still out there and still capable of killing someone else, regardless of what your bullshit theories are. Three, you got a guy who did you a favor, a guy who went to St. Alma's Church so you could traipse away for a few weeks. You got this guy named Michael Doherty who is dead as in dead and you don't give a shit. Well, I'm fed up with that shit."

Lieutenant Schmidt thought to say something to Terry Flynn but didn't. He remained seated.

Father Conklin suddenly sat down again.

"My God, don't you think I have guilt feelings about Michael? I have them every day. He's in my prayers every night. And in my dreams."

"So what are you going to do about him?"

Silence. Even the continuous roar of traffic along Lake Shore Drive could not penetrate this apartment. Terry Flynn stared at the priest.

117

"A few days ago—" he began.

Terry Flynn waited.

"A few days ago, a man came to confession. I was hearing confessions in St. Alma's."

"He confessed he killed Michael Doherty," Terry Flynn said.

"Yes. Not in the sacrament of Penance. I am not betraying his confidence or my vow of silence. He came in to explain it to me. He said he was a policeman, he had once taken a course at the university, and somehow he had the idea that I was his enemy—"

"He took a course from you?"

"Yes."

"When?"

"I don't know. He didn't tell me."

"Did you recognize him?"

"It was too dark."

"Did you recognize the voice? Anything? Black or white?"

"It was too dark," the priest said, unconsciously pushing his body away from the questions and into the false security of the large white pillows of the couch.

"Bullshit. Did he talk white or black?"

"Really," the priest began. "This is the kind of prejudicial—"

"Why don't you answer the question, Father?" Lieutenant Schmidt said quietly, easing into the expected role that Terry Flynn had forced on him a moment before by breaking the glass angel. He was the mild, friendly policeman now, a man of reason; Flynn would play the aggressor, the man of potential violence.

118

"I can't really say. I suppose he didn't talk with an urban black accent. That doesn't mean anything. He could be white or black. He could have been Spanish-speaking—"

"Why did he want to kill you?"

"He didn't say."

"Aw, come on, Father," Lieutenant Schmidt began in exasperation.

The brilliant blue eyes of the priest suddenly flashed angrily. "I am telling you the truth. He talked to me for fifteen minutes. He just talked and talked. He rambled on about everything and he said he had come to the church on that Monday morning to scare me, and at the last moment he realized he had a pistol in his hand and he shot Father Doherty without even being aware of it. I'm telling you the truth. I said to him, 'Why did you want to kill me?' And he said, 'You don't want to ask me that question. You don't want to know anything about me.' And it scared me, I admit it, it scared me when he talked like that. I was terrified of him. I thought he might shoot me right in the confessional."

"Look, in fifteen minutes he must have said a lot of things that gave you some idea who was talking to you—"

"My God, Lieutenant, I have two courses a quarter to teach, six a year, I have nearly four hundred undergraduates a year. In six years, that's over two thousand students. And graduate students I advise—nearly twenty a year. And then there's my work with the Criminal Justice Center at the University. I'm working with undergraduate and graduate students from a number of disciplines. I thought about it all the while he was talking to me. I felt like a butterfly pinned to a chart but still alive, though I couldn't move a muscle. It was a horrible experience."

"What did he smell like?" Lieutenant Schmidt said.

"What?"

"Smell. In a confessional box, it's very dark and the deprivation of vision enhances other senses. Smell is one. You're more keenly aware of odors, of human smells. What did he smell like?"

For a moment Father Bill Conklin closed his eyes as though to re-create the darkness of those fifteen minutes listening to the rambling conversation of the killer in the confessional of St. Alma's Catholic Church. The two detectives said nothing. The absolute silence of the apartment was stifling. Both detectives seemed almost to hold their breaths.

"Whisky," the priest said. "A very slight odor. Maybe it wasn't whisky. He didn't sound drunk to me. He said he had been drunk the morning he went to the church to scare me and killed Father Doherty. Maybe it wasn't whisky. Maybe it was vodka. Vodka has an odor, too, despite what they say. It was very slight—"

"Had he been drinking on the job the night before the mass?" Lieutenant Schmidt asked.

Father Conklin locked his hands together and then pulled at his right knee as though to draw it up into a defensive position across his lower body. "He didn't speak about that, about the job. He just said he was a policeman. He said—this is almost verbatim, I think—he said, 'You don't want to know any more about my job.'"

"Twice," Terry Flynn said.

The priest and the lieutenant looked at him. Flynn was looking away from them, staring at the shattered remains of the glass angel on the table, staring back at his own memory:

"Twice he said something like, 'You don't want to know blah-blah-blah.' Once when you asked him about being a student, once when he was talking about being a policeman. That's tough-guy talk. That's white talk too. You don't hear blacks talking that jive."

Matthew Schmidt permitted himself a thin smile of satisfaction. When he had picked Terry Flynn for the Special Squad, Commander Ranallo of Homicide had questioned his judgment, but Schmidt had thought he perceived more than the mere bluster and edgy toughness of a street-smart tactical cop. "He is a diamond in the rough," Schmidt had told Ranallo. "He just needs polishing." And Ranallo had replied, "Me, I think he's strictly dime-store glass, but it's your funeral."

Now, Matthew Schmidt thought, Flynn had again confirmed his conviction. "You have a point," Schmidt said quietly, and turned back to the priest. "We're going to need a statement, Father—"

"Look, what I've told you people must be held in confidence—"

"If you mean will we leak it to the media, the answer is no. But there is no such thing as an off-the-record remark. Not now. A man has been indicted for a crime you know he didn't commit—"

"That's not true. I don't know if it might have been Delford—"

"Father, we're not accusing you of anything. But you

121

had information vital to an investigation—a homicide investigation—and you withheld it. We will have a statement and we will have access to your student lists and we will question you." Matthew Schmidt let the words fall slowly, as gravely as the law.

And still the daydreams of Monday did not end. At a press conference held in the Civic Center offices of the state's attorney of Cook County, Bud Halligan, the amiable state's attorney, announced that justice was triumphant in the matter of Patrolman Delford. It was shortly before 3:00 P.M., in time for the final editions of the *Chicago Daily News* and the early editions of the *Chicago Sun-Times* and *Chicago Tribune*. The television stations had their cameras ready to record the planned event for showing on the five o'clock local news programs.

"As I have said before, our office seeks justice for all, regardless of race, color, or creed, and regardless of whether the accused is a policeman or a city official or someone who thinks he is beyond the normal scrutiny of the law," Bud Halligan said, reading the words prepared for him by Lee Horowitz. "We have moved swiftly in this matter and those groups who think that we have condoned police brutality should be made aware of it."

It was a wonderful press conference and might have continued to be a wonderful day except for the call made to Lee Horowitz at home shortly after 6:00 P.M. The caller was Jack Donovan of the Criminal Division. He said that Father William Conklin had made a statement to the

122

police in the presence of his own attorney and a representative of the state's attorney's office.

"So what the hell are you telling me, Jack?" Horowitz demanded as he stood at the telephone located on a sideboard to the left of his dining room table. "What are you dropping on me?"

"If Conklin is right, then the indictment of Delford for the murder of Father Doherty is wrong," Jack Donovan said with some satisfaction in his voice.

"I want to read that statement, I want to read that fucking statement right now—"

"It's being typed. It'll be ready in an hour or so," Jack Donovan said mildly.

"Goddammit, Jack, you just ruined my dinner," Lee Horowitz said.

"I'm sorry," Donovan said. But the tone of his voice did not carry a note of regret.

14
CUTTING THE DEAL

"**S**o what do we have here?"

But nobody had to answer Lee Horowitz's question. It was a mess and it was going to make everyone look bad.

"We might even lose Delford on the rape now," Mario DeVito said glumly.

They were in the office of the chief of the Criminal Division of the state's attorney's office. It was shortly before midnight on the strange Monday they would all remember. Matthew Schmidt and Terry Flynn had finished questioning Father Conklin in the presence of Jack Donovan and a Loop attorney named Magis, who represented the priest. The statement had been typed and signed four hours before.

A copy of the statement lay on Jack Donovan's uncluttered desk. Donovan was, as usual, not seated at the desk but propped against the ledge of the second-floor window in the office that opened on a light well. Mario DeVito, who had presented the case against Delford to the grand jury just that morning, was sprawled on the couch, his tie loosened, his belly straining against the slightly gray fabric of a shirt that had been white at nine this morning. He wasn't tired, he merely felt defeated; this is the way he would have explained it to Jack Donovan if Lee Horowitz had not been present in the office.

"This is going to kill Bud," Lee said for the fourteenth time in the past two hours. "Absolutely kill him."

The other two men did not speak.

"And what about the cops?"

"The cops are easy. What about the fallout from the Cardinal's office?"

"The Cardinal wanted an arrest," Lee Horowitz said, as though defending the idea of ecumenical alliances in the law. "We gave him an arrest. Now we got to take it back."

"There's no way out," Mario DeVito agreed and yawned.

"Poor Bud," Lee Horowitz said.

"Poor us," Mario DeVito said.

Jack Donovan, who had spoken rarely since the interview with Father Conklin, now cleared his throat in the dry atmosphere of the stuffy room. "We don't do anything," Jack Donovan said.

Lee and Mario stared at him.

"Jack, I never thought I'd hear that from you," Mario said at last in a mocking tone. "You getting chicken in your old age?"

But Jack Donovan was not listening. He had figured it out and now he wanted to put it in words before the idea evaporated.

"We leave Delford where he is. He's awaiting trial, he can wait it out in jail. He's a convicted armed robber, a rogue cop, a rapist." The words were delivered without vehemence.

"But not a murderer," Mario DeVito said.

"Yes," Jack Donovan replied. "That's the point. There still is a priest-killer out there somewhere. And now that we have the wrong man, perhaps he can be encouraged to come out of the closet."

Lee Horowitz said nothing, afraid to interrupt the monologue and lose the thought that was developing.

"If we spring Delford and quash the murder indictment, we scare the killer into his closet. In the statement, Father Conklin said the killer has remorse, has a need to confess, to explain. Now that we have a suspect in County Jail, the remorse should increase."

"So what?" Mario DeVito said. He sat up suddenly on the couch. "This is shit, Jack, and you know it. You talk like Lee does. We indicted the wrong guy. It's an indictment, not a conviction. We pull it back. Easy enough."

"No, it's not so easy," Jack Donovan said. He glanced up at Lee. "Is it, Lee?"

"No," Lee Horowitz replied, beginning to understand. "We say that Delford didn't kill the priest, we still got all the heat in the world on us. Heat from the Fifth Floor, heat from the cops, heat from the Cardinal. But if we say nothing, there's no heat."

126

"And in the meantime, how can you get the killer?" Mario DeVito asked. "You're putting a lot of faith in cops, Jack. You're a lawyer, not a cop, you ought to know better."

"I was a cop," Jack Donovan said.

"So what? I used to be an altar boy. That don't make me a priest now. We go to court at the end of the month, that's two weeks away. What do we do then? We ask for a continuance? You can't keep a guy in the shithouse just because you can't take a little heat."

Jack Donovan felt queasy again. His stomach ached and a sort of nausea seemed to fill his nostrils. He rubbed his belly absently; he didn't even know it was considered a characteristic gesture in the office. Everything he had just told Mario and Lee went against his own judgment, his own idea of right and wrong. He was not a politician; he had a sense of the fairness of the law buried under layers of indifference and cynicism that papered the whole system. And yet he thought he was doing the right thing now; it was the only way.

"Let me have until morning, until I can talk to Matt Schmidt and see what he thinks," Jack Donovan said.

"Hey, you don't need my permission to be an asshole," Mario DeVito said.

"You're the asshole," Lee Horowitz said with sudden savageness. The feisty first assistant got to his feet. He turned from Mario to Jack Donovan. "You got the time and more."

"What if Father Conklin goes talking about this?"

"Father Conklin isn't going to shit without permission," Lee Horowitz said. "He's in a lot of fucking trouble, that priest. He withheld evidence vital to an investigation, he obstructed, we got his nuts in a wringer—"

"That's not a nice way to talk about the clergy," Mario DeVito said.

"Nice? Listen, I respect your religion—"

"*Mazel tov,*" said Mario DeVito with a sudden smile, and Lee Horowitz wondered if he was being made the butt of a joke.

"You got some idea, Jack?" Horowitz said.

"One idea. Not much of an idea but I want to see what Matt Schmidt thinks about it."

"What is it?"

"Oh, nothing complicated."

"Maybe I don't want to know about it," Lee Horowitz said.

Jack Donovan considered that remark seriously for a moment and then looked at the other two men in the midnight-bright room.

"No," he said slowly. "Maybe it would be better if you didn't know what it was."

15

A MATTER FOR CONFESSION

At ten o'clock on Tuesday morning, Jack Donovan spoke privately with Lieutenant Matthew Schmidt of the Homicide/Rape Division for more than an hour across a table littered with breakfast remains at Lou Mitchell's on Jackson. The place was an ancient meeting ground for cops in plain clothes and lawyers and federal agents who shared coffee and secrets. Jack Donovan had a long secret and Matthew Schmidt did not interrupt him as he unveiled it.

"There are risks," Schmidt said at last.

"Physical, you mean, or the other kind?"

"There's always physical risks, but the other kind, I can't assign someone to the other kind."

Jack Donovan stared at the older man for a moment. Donovan's face was hard now, reflecting a sense of stubborn sureness that was usually foreign to him. He had held out against indicting Delford for murder as long as he could, and in the end it wasn't good enough. He had felt weak all Monday because of his failure, but with the startling revelations of Father Conklin about the rambling discourse of a killer, he had come awake again and been energized by it.

"These are cops you are talking about," Jack Donovan said. "I was a cop."

"But you aren't anymore," Matt Schmidt said. "Ranallo would love to cut off Terry Flynn's balls with a big butcher knife. And Margolies . . . well, Margolies knows how to take care of himself."

"And Karen Kovac," Jack Donovan said.

"Yes," Matt Schmidt said. "I suppose I would have to bring her in. And if it blows up in our face, Ranallo never has been crazy about the idea of a female in Homicide."

"And you?"

"I don't care," Matt Schmidt said slowly, staring at the remains of the coffee in the cup in front of him. "You know that. I can retire anytime. I don't need shit from anyone."

"I admit it's a gamble," Jack Donovan said.

"I'll put it to them," Matt Schmidt said.

"I'd like to be there," Donovan said.

"All right, Jack. I suppose that would be fair. But I'm going to tell them the risks. All of the risks."

And Matt Schmidt did tell them.

The meeting was held at five in the afternoon in the

crowded little office they shared on the sixth floor of police headquarters. The building was under unusually heavy guard that morning because someone had called in a threat to bomb the statue of a policeman in the lobby of the building. The statue, which had once stood on a promontory overlooking the Dan Ryan Expressway, had been moved to the relative security of police headquarters after radicals had bombed it three times in the late 1960s. The statue commemorated the policemen killed in the Haymarket Riot, nearly a century before, which was now marked each year in socialist countries by the holiday called May Day.

"Do we tell the pastor of St. Alma's what we're doing?"

"No," Jack Donovan said.

"Why not?" asked Sid Margolies. "It's his church. What if we shot it up?"

"What if the old man said no? What if he said he had to check with the chancery office and got the Cardinal on our case again?" Jack Donovan said. "The only guy who has to know is Father Conklin, and we've got him in our pocket."

Terry Flynn had said nothing during the meeting, but now he smiled broadly. "I love it. I always wanted to play a priest."

"This isn't a joke," said Lieutenant Schmidt.

Terry Flynn kept grinning. "I'm going to hear confessions. What do you figure people are confessing these days?"

"I don't like this," Karen Kovac said. "I'm not a Catholic. I don't practice my religion anymore anyway—"

"You're a fallen-away Catholic," Terry Flynn said, still grinning.

"This isn't funny to me. How do you keep people who want to go to confession away from the church?"

"We don't," said Jack Donovan. "But I see your problem. Tell you what we can do. We see old ladies coming in to have their confessions heard, we can steer them away from the confession area. Father Conklin can use one of the other confessionals in the back of the church."

"This is complicated," Sid Margolies complained. "I'm supposed to be some guy praying in Christian—"

Terry Flynn couldn't stand it. He laughed out loud. "I love this. I want to see Sid in a Catholic church, making the Stations of the Cross."

"Listen, Terry, I don't like to make fun of religion."

"I know, it's a holy subject."

Schmidt glanced sharply at Flynn, who caught the look and let the grin suffice instead of words.

"We position Sid at one of the Stations along the wall of the right side of the church," Jack Donovan said. "We put Karen in a pew opposite the confessionals. And Terry is in the box."

"And wired," Terry Flynn said.

"Yes," said Jack Donovan. "If you all agree with this, I can go to Judge O'Brien. He owes me a few and he'll do the court order. I want this airtight."

"And what makes you think the shooter is going to come to surface again?" Sid Margolies said.

"I don't know. I can't give you a reason. Just read Father Conklin's statement and tell me what you think."

"In the meantime," Sid persisted, "you have someone locked up who isn't guilty of the crime he's charged with."

"Oh, cut the shit, Sid," Terry Flynn said. "Delford is a mope. Since when did you get elected to the American Civil Liberties Union?"

"I happen to belong to the ACLU," Sid said, and no one was very much surprised by the statement. Sid Margolies was not a usual sort to be a policeman, a fact that had attracted Matthew Schmidt's attention when he was putting together the Special Squad.

"This is just a fishing expedition, isn't it?" Karen Kovac said. Her voice was so quiet that it commanded the attention of everyone in the room.

After a moment, Jack Donovan nodded his head.

"And nobody knows about it, do they?"

"Nobody," Jack Donovan answered.

"It can only work if Delford is still under arrest," she said. "But if the shooter doesn't show up at confession, you're going to have to let Delford go."

Jack Donovan waited.

"Did this priest, Father Conklin, release his student records at last?" she asked. Donovan understood. She didn't like the wild chance element of his plan—if you could call it a plan at all. Policemen try to avoid theories and psychological guesses for fear of missing the mundane motive lying in front of them. A year ago, Karen Kovac would not have questioned the plan. But now she knew more; she was more of a cop.

"This morning," said Matt Schmidt. "I've gone through it. There are nearly three thousand names and grades. By going through all the student lists and comparing them with departmental lists, we could probably have all the police officers' names in a week. We're not in the computer age yet." He made a face. "If it was a policeman."

"Come on. It had to be a cop," Terry Flynn said.

"No," Matt Schmidt replied. "He said he was a policeman and we assume he was telling the truth."

"And he talked like a policeman," Terry Flynn said.

"How do policemen talk?" Sid Margolies asked.

"Tough," Terry Flynn said. "You know, someone asks you where the Art Institute is, you say, 'You don't want to know, honey.'"

They smiled. For some reason, it was the right thing for Flynn to say. A sort of queasy tenseness in the room settled down.

"And motive," Matt Schmidt said. "We get the cop names and try to pin a motive on them. And we assume the shooter is crazy, so his motive is crazy too. No. We need too many people for that. I couldn't hide the manpower from Ranallo, he'd ask me what I was doing with so many people."

"The only reason we don't tell Ranallo the investigation is still on is to save Bud Halligan's ass, is that it?" asked Terry Flynn, looking directly at Jack Donovan. The tension Flynn had dissipated a moment before was back; usually, there was little love lost between detectives and the lawyers from the state's attorney's office. The police usually thought the prosecutors were lacking in the zeal necessary to convict criminals the police knew were guilty; the prosecutors usually thought the police were too dumb or lazy to come up with sufficient evidence to make a case. Now Flynn had stated the unspoken thought at the core of the reluctance of the detectives to adopt the plan; somehow they felt trapped by the plan because it came from the SAO.

"Yes," said Jack Donovan.

"No," said Matthew Schmidt, shifting in his chair to face Terry Flynn, who was leaning against a filing cabinet. "To save our ass as well. The moment we let Delford off the hook, we get heat again from Ranallo and the superintendent and the Cardinal, which is not to mention the Fifth Floor at the Hall. I don't need that heat and I didn't see you sunbathing in it either, Terry, when I found you wallowing up to your chin in this case."

"I just hate letting an asshole like Bud Halligan off the hook," Terry Flynn said with a fierce grin.

"Maybe Jack hates letting a loudmouth like you get out of the slops," Matt Schmidt said.

And Sid Margolies laughed aloud at that, which was very strange because Sid rarely smiled at anything, let alone laughed. They all stared at him until he was finished.

When he had finished laughing, no one said anything for a moment.

"I'm glad you think it's funny," Terry Flynn said at last.

"It's tragic," Sid Margolies said. "What are you going to do except laugh?"

Nobody had an answer.

16
BEFORE THE STORM

They were both off Friday. At times, they would not share a day off for weeks because of the differences in their schedules and would snatch a few hours here and there to see each other between shifts. But they had the whole day Friday, and it felt as empty and luxurious as a Saturday morning in childhood.

Terry Flynn called her at nine. Karen Kovac was still in bed and her voice sounded sleepy and husky. He called it her sexy voice and that pleased her because she had never thought of her way of speaking as sexy.

"The temperature is going to be sixty and it is bright and sunny," Terry Flynn said in imitation of a radio weatherman. "How about a picnic in the Arboretum?"

"Isn't it too cold?"

"I'll bring a blanket."

"You and blankets. You must have a dozen blankets."

"Ten, actually," he said. "Souvenirs of my army days. The U.S. Army has the finest blankets in the world."

"A picnic," she said, smiling at the thought of it. It had been years since she had been to a picnic.

"It's not like you to come up with an idea like this," she said in her teasing half-whisper.

"I'm a very romantic fellow," he said. "Besides, I like the country. In small doses, that is."

"Should I make something?"

"Just me," he said. "I'll go over to Klein's Deli and get the fixings. And the beer."

"Beer is not romantic enough," she said. "I'll bring a bottle of wine."

"You can't have wine with corned beef on onion rolls."

"I can't think about food before noon," she said.

"And kosher dills," Terry Flynn said. "I had some leftover pizza for breakfast this morning. I think I like cold pizza better than hot."

"Ugh," she said. "Get what you want, I'll wait for you."

They drove to the Morton Arboretum in the western suburbs. It was nearly deserted because it was a weekday. Terry Flynn drove through the gate off Route 59 and followed the narrow roadway into the thickening woods that broke as suddenly as morning to reveal a hidden meadow and a small lake, fringed with autumn trees. They parked the car in a secluded lot and walked along the paths between the stands of trees, down to the lake. The maples had all turned, and the stands of trees glowed red and fierce yellow in the slight wind. She wore a wool sweater and he wore a White Sox jacket.

She took his arm; he jammed his hands in the pockets of the jacket. They walked along a path that wound around the lake. They passed an elderly couple taking photographs of the lake and the stands of trees. The sky was bright blue.

"This is so beautiful, so peaceful," Karen Kovac said, hugging his arm.

"Yeah. Every time I do this kind of thing, I think I want to live in the country. But it's a lie. If I lived in the country, I'd shoot myself. You should visit the country, but don't live there."

"This is only the suburbs," she said.

"But this place is like the country," Terry Flynn said. "The suburbs. I'd go crazy in the suburbs."

"You go crazy in the city," she said, teasing him again.

"Yeah, I know, but I can get out once in a while and clear my sinuses. But living out here, I know I'd never get into the city. Nobody does. It makes you lazy. One of my buddies moved out to Elmhurst ten years ago and now I never see him. He never gets into town. He works in town, in the Loop, but right at 5:43 or something, he's on the train to Elmhurst. On the weekends, he cuts grass. Shit, he used to smoke the stuff and now he cuts it. People get dulled out in the suburbs. I'd rather stay alive."

"Be careful," she said.

"What? About what? I ain't moving to the suburbs."

"Tomorrow," she said.

"You mean when I become a priest?" It was his turn to tease her but she wasn't smiling.

138

They walked under a stand of maples. Their shoes crunched through the leaves. Karen Kovac felt overwhelmingly nostalgic in that moment, and that led to sadness. She could not explain it, even to herself.

"We wait until he comes out of the box to take him," Terry Flynn said. "He isn't going to shoot me in the box. After all, I'm a priest."

"Be careful," she said again.

"Listen, did you know that confessional boxes are bulletproof in the ghetto?"

"Oh, don't make everything a joke. I don't like this idea at all."

"Neither do I. But I like the idea of Ranallo on my ass every day even less. And if I never see another priest again, it'll be too soon."

"Like Father Conklin."

"What an asshole. I read that book of his you gave me. He's like every priest I ever met. He doesn't know shit about anything. He said in there that the way to cure the recidivism rate was to close more prisons, that the prison itself led to the problem of repeat offenders—"

"Not that simply," she said, and found it odd to defend the priest.

"No? You tell me what he said, then."

"He's saying that prison life alters a person's psychological profile, that he not only thinks like a criminal in prison but that he unconsciously longs to return to prison, the prison is a womb for him after he leaves. . . ."

"Crap. This is crap," Terry Flynn said. "When you catch criminals, you lock them up. That is sensible. You do not put them on probation, you do not pat them on the head, you do not say, 'Go and sin no more.' You put them in the shithouse and you throw away the key. You do not worry about their psychological profile."

"You just want to fight with me," Karen Kovac said, because she knew Terry Flynn. Part of his abrasiveness was to hide his sensitivity. Something bothered him now. Perhaps he was afraid.

"I never fight. I'm a lover."

"The leaves are so beautiful, it makes you want to say something that's not just saying how beautiful everything is."

They crossed a bridge over the lake and now they were in a wide, gently sloping meadow that led up to a stand of evergreens. They traipsed across the dried, brown grass of the meadow.

"When I was a kid, I was an altar boy. I wanted to be a priest for a while. Every kid wants to be a priest for a while, I guess."

"Not Sid Margolies," Karen Kovac said.

Terry Flynn smiled. "I was about fifteen, it was this time of year, and one day I just realized I not only didn't want to be a priest anymore, I didn't want anything to do with them. I stopped being Catholic. My mother didn't know. Well, maybe she did know but I thought I fooled her. I'd go out on Sunday morning to go to Mass but I went over to Walgreen's drugstore and had a cheeseburger instead. We used to call it St. Walgreen's."

"You lost your faith," she said.

"Maybe I never had any," he said. "Maybe I was like the old man. He was a Catholic, a great guy to hang around at golf outings with the Monsignor and put a hundred in the collection basket every Christmas, except it was a hundred he got as part of the shakedown in the district. I ever tell you my old man even had a diamond pinkie ring? Like a fucking alderman."

"Your father's dead. Don't talk about him," she said quietly.

"I know. I usually don't. But I was thinking about it all night. We used to live in St. Alma's before the colored moved in. I was really a little kid, maybe eight or nine. I was bored to tears at Mass on Sunday. The old man led us to the twelve o'clock Mass and sat there in his three-piece suit and his pinkie ring and then, after Mass, he'd have a few words in the sacristy with the Monsignor. What a couple of phonies."

"You don't like priests because you don't like your father," she said. They had reached the top of the meadow and were under the stand of trees.

"No," he said, and he looked at her. His features were flat, his eyes without depth, his voice very low.

"You're wrong, Karen. I loved him."

They made love in the car in the woods, hidden from the road by trees. She protested at first. She said it was silly to make love in an automobile when they could return to the city and make love on a comfortable bed. It was silly, he agreed.

After they made love, they pulled up their clothes awkwardly in the confined space. They sat for a long time next to each other, sipping the last of the beer. The bright day had long since disappeared; early-afternoon clouds had convened and now it began to rain.

Terry Flynn got out of the car and stood for a moment in the rain. The rain was cold but gentle. The trees shielded him from some of the rain. He listened to the rain striking the leaves on the trees around him. The rain and wind played the trees like instruments playing a gentle childhood song.

17

A MAN IS WATCHING

Evening.

Father William Conklin crossed the quadrangle within the hollow of the old Gothic buildings of the University of Chicago.

It was a gentle fall evening. The trees were mostly shed of their leaves, and the old elms and oaks seemed suited to this time of year and time of evening. They added an ancient quality to the stone buildings, which were imitations of ancient European university structures.

Lights from the buildings were subdued, as were the lights across the paths of the quad. The university sprawled in the comfortable old neighborhood of Hyde Park, floating in the midst of the black ghetto of the South Side and yet serenely independent from it, like a cruise ship sailing on a dangerous sea.

Father Conklin shivered in the chill of the early-evening

air. It was too cold too soon, he thought, as he had thought all the first autumn nights of his life.

He had spent the afternoon pondering his own death.

Which of them had wanted him dead? he thought, as he stared at records scattered on his desk. He had tried to see their faces, matching names and features in his mind.

No, he had realized after an hour; he could not remember. He could not really remember any of them.

He scarcely noticed the figure coming along the path behind him.

The city surged outside this island of academic calm, but here it was dark, lonely.

He heard the steps of the other on the walk and turned for a moment. Two weeks before, he would not have thought to turn.

A policeman.

He had stopped and the other had stopped as well.

Should he speak?

He turned instead and cut across the lawn to a place between Ida Noyes Hall and an adjacent building. In a few moments he was on the Midway, a wide parkway with a grassy incline on four sides depressing the park land beneath the level of street traffic.

He was due at the Institute of Criminology Research, across the Midway, at seven.

He had taken this path many times.

He walked down the incline and started across the grass and turned once and saw the policeman in uniform standing on the walkway 150 feet behind him.

O my God, I am heartily sorry . . .

The words of confession came as automatically as the thought of his death, the thought he had been pondering all afternoon.

No life is blameless. We all need God's mercy.

So the old priest had counseled in the seminary, and the words had not been recalled by Father Conklin for fifteen years. He was with sin but not without hope of salvation . . .

O my God. But the words stuck in his mind.

He realized he was running across the dried autumn field. A quiet wind scattered brown leaves before him in the dim evening light.

And then he heard the footsteps behind him running.

He realized he was going to die. He realized he was terribly afraid of the thought of his own death.

"Please," a voice said and he was surprised that it was his own.

He stumbled on the far side of the field and fell against the grassy slope and then rose, scrambling up to the sidewalk.

He ran between parked cars into Midway Plaisance and was nearly struck by a CTA bus that slammed on its brakes.

He didn't stop.

Up the steps of the Institute. He banged against the glass doors. They were locked, as were all the university buildings on this side of the Midway, which bordered a savage neighborhood called Woodlawn. He banged his hands against the triple-thick glass doors and felt suddenly part of a nightmare.

In the light of the foyer, he saw the outline of a university security guard. He pressed his body against the glass.

The guard stared at him strangely for a moment and then recognized him and pressed the entry buzzer.

"What's wrong, Father?"

Conklin fell into the foyer, breathing hard, his face white.

"Someone out there . . . someone chasing me—"

The guard pulled his pistol and opened the door.

He stared out at Midway Plaisance and the grassy field beyond and the Gothic buildings of the core of the university on the far side.

"I don't see no one, Father—"

"A man—" And then he stopped. Could he say a man dressed as a policeman? It was absurd. There was no threat against him. He couldn't speak. Who wanted to kill him?

"Father, I'll call for a car but I don't see anyone now. Where was he?"

"Behind me . . . coming across—"

The black guard turned to look at the ashen face of the priest. "Colored guy?"

"I didn't see," Father Conklin said.

"Had a woman attacked, her purse ripped off, a couple of hours ago around by the Law Library."

And Father Conklin stared at the security guard with the drawn pistol as though he had never seen the man before. Madness, he thought with great and horrible clarity. We live in madness, anarchy, chaos, and we accept it just as this security guard accepts it. His death was not so unthinkable after all.

146

He was always aware of the effect of his uniform. It pleased him. He finished the dregs of the cup of coffee and replaced the cup on the saucer. He picked up a paper napkin and wiped his mouth and reached for the bill. He dropped a quarter on the counter and the waitress smiled at him. He smiled back at her. He felt ten feet tall. He always felt this way in uniform.

He climbed off the swivel stool and took the check across the linoleum floor to the checker at the glass cigar counter. He pulled a dollar bill out of his pocket.

"No, that's all right," said the old Greek. "I like you guys to come in here at night. You want a refill? Piece of pie?"

"No. Not tonight. Got to roll," he said. He didn't smile or acknowledge the freebie except to nod slightly, exactly as a movie hero might nod at one of the frightened townspeople lining the wooden sidewalk, thankful for his presence.

He touched the pistol on his belt and zipped his leather jacket. He took the blue eggshell helmet from beneath his arm and placed it on his head. He knew exactly what he looked like, he knew exactly how he felt at that moment as all eyes watched him. He was part of the thin blue line holding back the tide of evil ready to spill into their solid, dull lives and drown them.

He pushed open the door of the little restaurant on Fifty-fifth Street and walked outside. The night air was cold and bracing.

He had only wanted to speak to the priest.

Outside the confessional.

To explain the hurt the priest had done him.

To explain.

He stared at the denizens of the shabby street, moving back and forth like dreamers beneath the bright signlights.

He could have done so much if the priest hadn't screwed up everything for him. The priest didn't even know what he'd done.

You don't want to know.

But it wasn't enough, not for him. He wanted to tell the priest now. He wanted him to know, to realize how carelessly he had ruined a man's life.

The man in the police uniform smiled.

Not tonight but maybe tomorrow. He'd tell the priest, let him suffer knowing everything he had done.

And then he would kill the right man this time.

18
PRIESTLY MURDER

After it was over, Jack Donovan realized he should have seen the major flaw in his plan. But none of them had seen it until it was too late.

Terry Flynn unlocked the door of the confessional box at 2:45 P.M. Saturday and went inside. It was small, containing a single hard chair and a light activated by a chain pull. He turned on the light and adjusted the tape recorder fixed to his belt and then the microphone pinned to his shirt. They had decided there was no need to hide the microphone under the shirt because the room would be dark when the suspect entered the confessional. If he entered it at all.

Karen Kovac wore a long dark coat and her face and head were partially covered with a babushka tied under her chin. She had a rosary in her hand. Under her coat she wore a .32-caliber Smith & Wesson pistol in a leather holster. In her black purse in the pew beside her was a second pistol, a .22-caliber Smith & Wesson sneak gun.

Forty feet away, in an aisle leading to the confessional box, Sid Margolies stared up solemnly at a mosaic on the wall depicting the Fourth Station of the Cross. It portrayed Christ falling beneath the burden of the cross he is carrying to his own execution. It was one of fourteen Stations of the Cross arrayed throughout the church to commemorate moments in the passion and death of Jesus Christ.

Sid Margolies carried a .357 Magnum in a clip holster at his waist. His coat was open and he could remove the pistol and cock and fire it in less than two seconds.

Matthew Schmidt was seated behind the door leading to the sacristy. He held a pistol in his right hand, already cocked. It was his venerable .44 Colt with the long barrel. In twenty-nine years on the force, he had used the pistol exactly once, in a firefight with two armed robbers emerging from a currency exchange. The two robbers had been killed along with an elderly woman passerby caught in the crossfire. Because Schmidt was one of six policemen firing, he was not sure until the autopsies which bullet had killed the passerby. He had felt immense relief and some guilt when the autopsy report indicated the robbers had shot the passerby, not the policemen. No one at the time had understood his mixed feelings about the incident.

Terry Flynn turned in the box and sat down on the hard chair and placed the revolver on his lap. He glanced at Karen Kovac in the pew opposite him and smiled. She turned and looked at him.

"I'm going to be giving out some heavy penances today," Terry Flynn said, holding the pistol up.

She smiled despite herself. "Be quiet, Terry, and close that door."

He grinned like a schoolboy out on a prank and did as he was told.

And they waited.

It was decided at the last minute that Father Bill Conklin should not be in the church at all. There was an element of risk for him, as Karen Kovac had pointed out. Jack Donovan had taken up a station inside the vestibule of the church, between the heavy outer doors and the inner doors. He was in an office at the end of the vestibule and could watch those who came in and left. Twice he stopped elderly women about to enter the church for confessions and told them that the time of confessions had been set back until six that night. The women agreed to return.

At 3:14 P.M., a large young man in the uniform of a Chicago motorcycle policeman opened the outer door and stepped into the vestibule. He did not look right or left but straight ahead.

Jack Donovan pulled a pistol from his holster. He was an attorney and had no use for guns anymore; the pistol was a relic of his eight years on the police force. He had cleaned and oiled it the night before. He told none of them about the pistol because he felt curiously ashamed of carrying it on this assignment. He was in no danger.

The policeman in an eggshell helmet and black leather jacket pushed open the inner door and entered the church. He glanced at the woman kneeling in the pew next to the confessional. He did not notice Sid Margolies until he walked past him. Sid Margolies was moving his lips as in prayer; in fact, he was praying, but in Hebrew.

The policeman walked to the middle of the church and pushed open the door of the confessional without removing his helmet.

He knelt on the kneeler, which lit a small green signal light outside the box and one in the cubicle occupied by Terry Flynn.

Terry Flynn picked up the pistol and pushed open the small sliding panel over the window that separated the two boxes. He barely saw a figure in the darkness, half-hidden by the screen between them.

"Conklin?"

The priestly figure nodded in the half darkness.

"You know me," the kneeling figure said, and Terry Flynn nodded again slightly.

"You know that this man didn't kill that priest, this man they have in jail," the figure said. "You let him stay in jail. You call yourself a criminologist and you're a priest, but you're as much to blame as I am for what happened."

Terry Flynn put a handkerchief to his nose and spoke through the muffled cloth to disguise his voice. "Why did you want to kill me when you killed Father Doherty?"

"You still don't understand? You still don't understand? My God, you did it to yourself, Conklin. You killed me. What did I ever want in my life except to be a policeman? And when you filed that report, you put me back so far I knew I never would become a policeman.

You lied to them about me, about my lack of maturity—that's what they told me. They turned me down. You killed every chance I could have had."

Terry Flynn sat perfectly still. He said nothing.

"Do you know what I think? You're a coward," the kneeling figure said. "I should have done this last week just to let them know. I should have done it last week."

"Done what?"

"Kill you. I kill you now and they'll know they got the wrong man."

"You don't want to kill anyone. You told me that last week."

"That was last week," the figure said. "I been thinking about it all week and the more I been thinking about it, the more I know I gotta kill you."

Terry Flynn let the handkerchief fall from his face. He moved his hand slowly to the pistol on his lap and then, in the darkness, did a clumsy thing. He bumped the pistol off his lap.

It clattered on the linoleum floor and the kneeling figure flinched.

"I dropped something," Flynn said and bent down. His hand probed the floor. He couldn't find the pistol.

"Sit up. Sit up now or I'm shooting," the kneeling figure said.

There it was, Terry thought, under the chair.

Then he heard the ominous click of a revolver being cocked. There wasn't any time.

He sat up straight and waited. How ludicrous, he thought. He thought of Karen Kovac in the stands of maples and oaks at the Arboretum. Be careful, he thought.

"I want you to forgive me," the kneeling figure said.

"How can I forgive you when you want to kill me?" Terry Flynn said.

"Forgive me," he said and Terry Flynn saw the pistol raised near the level of the window. The barrel was pointed at him.

Terry Flynn raised his right hand as though in blessing and leaned back in the chair.

"Sit up," the kneeling figure said.

Terry Flynn kicked the door suddenly and it flew open and he pushed himself forward, out of the chair, just as the kneeling man fired.

The bullet struck him in the left buttock and was deflected into the wooden panel covering the window on the opposite side of the confessional.

Terry Flynn saw Karen Kovac turn in that moment, her shiny pistol already in hand.

Be careful. Be careful. The words seemed repeated a thousand times in his mind in that split second. She half rose in the pew.

Sid Margolies had his pistol out and was braced in the classic stance in the aisle.

Terry hit the floor of the church and rolled away, out of Karen's line of fire. As he rolled, the door of the confessional opened and the figure of a policeman in helmet and black leather jacket emerged, pistol in hand.

"Drop the piece, drop the piece," Karen Kovac shouted and her voice echoed in the eerie emptiness of the vast old church.

For a moment the police figure at the confessional door stood stock-still.

"Drop it!" shouted Sid Margolies. "Police!"

"I'm the police," the uniformed man said suddenly. "You're under arrest!"

"Drop the piece!" Margolies said.

The uniformed man looked from Margolies to Karen Kovac and back, as though deciding.

Matt Schmidt appeared in the aisle at the sacristy door. He held his .44 in front of him, not in the classic stance of firing arm braced at the wrist by the second arm but in a curiously old-fashioned gunfighter's stance. The big pistol was aimed belly high.

"This is a conspiracy against the police!" the uniformed man shouted. "All of you are under arrest!"

The four figures with drawn pistols stood motionless. Terry Flynn, on the floor, stared up at the uniformed man less than ten feet away. He felt sick to his stomach. Be careful. He thought of Karen Kovac walking under the maple trees and his father sitting in a pew at the twelve o'clock High Mass. He felt a burning sensation in his behind and wetness filling his trousers.

"Come on, Officer, you know the rules. Drop the pistol," Matt Schmidt said quietly.

It didn't work.

"Fuck you!" screamed the uniformed man and he whirled on Matt Schmidt and fired twice.

Karen's first shot hit him in the left shoulder.

Margolies's first shot splintered the wood of the confessional box and pierced a carved angel's head. The second shot struck the uniformed man in the spine.

155

The killer's third shot went off at the same moment the .44 in Matt Schmidt's hand boomed. The enormous slug ripped the killer open from ribs to scrotum.

He fell forward firing. He was dead as he squeezed the fourth shot. It went wild and chipped a piece of marble off the high altar in the center of the church.

The sounds of the shots continued for a moment after the body of the killer hit the floor, less than five feet from Terry Flynn. The still air of the church was filled with the acrid smell of gunpowder expended in a closed room. Karen's hand was suddenly shaking and she let the hand holding the pistol drop to her side.

Margolies held his stance for a moment, his pistol trained on the body of the killer. Just in case.

"Is everyone all right?" Jack Donovan asked. He was at the door of the church.

No one spoke for a moment.

"Okay," Karen Kovac said in a dull voice.

Matt Schmidt let his pistol hand drop, the gun still smoking. He started along the aisle. Sid Margolies dropped his pistol hand as well.

"Everyone okay?" Jack Donovan asked again.

"Well, actually, I got shot in the ass," said Terry Flynn. "My pants are all wet."

Karen's face went pale. She knelt beside him.

"I just hope it's blood," Terry Flynn said, and smiled.

19
MASS FOR THE DEAD

His name was Victor DeLeo and he had been wrong.

Not only about mistaking Father Doherty for Father Conklin. He had been wrong about not becoming a policeman.

Three weeks after the shooting in St. Alma's Catholic Church on Forty-seventh Street on the South Side of Chicago, it made sense of sorts.

"He used me as a reference when he made his application and I gave him a great recommendation," Father Bill Conklin said. "I didn't know him very well but I looked up his grades. He took two courses of mine. Got A's in both of them, and I can assure you I don't give out marks like that for not doing the work."

The statement of Father Conklin puzzled the detectives further until they got access to Victor DeLeo's file.

157

The turndown had come as a result of a profile obtained from the Department of Defense. DeLeo had served two tours in Vietnam and had been recommended for discharge by an obscure psychiatric physician working in a hospital for GIs in Saigon. The paperwork had moved so slowly that DeLeo had been honorably discharged before he would have been given a Section Eight discharge.

"Battle stress, emotional immaturity, alcoholism . . ." Matthew Schmidt explained to Terry Flynn, who was recovering from his wound at home. "Five years ago he applied for the class and we got this routine medical report from the service when we asked to confirm that he'd been honorably discharged. We didn't even want it but they sent it along because the Department of the Army screwed up its own files in St. Louis."

"Poor sonofabitch. It's like getting the wrong phone bill," Terry Flynn said.

"He was convinced that Father Conklin had provided the decisive blow against him but Conklin had nothing to do with it. Conklin always stressed the psychological makeup of policemen in his criminology classes, so DeLeo assumed that the priest had somehow crossed him when he asked him for a letter of recommendation. Naïve."

"No, Matt," Terry Flynn said. "Just sad. He let it fester and fester. He had a security job, wore a uniform, carried a piece, but it wasn't like being a cop. He bought those cop clothes. He wanted to be a real cop."

Matt Schmidt said nothing for a moment.

"This place is a mess," he said at last.

"Who are you? The man from *Better Homes and Gardens*?"

"Do you always sleep on the couch?"

"Yeah," Terry Flynn said. "I like it that way. That way, Karen invites me over to her apartment and does all the cooking. She cleaned the place up for me about a week ago, but I keep telling her it's hopeless."

"What's that on the wall?"

"That's where I throw the spaghetti to see if it's cooked right. When it sticks to the wall, it's cooked just enough."

Matthew Schmidt made a face. "That's disgusting."

"You ought to see the bathroom, you want to see disgusting."

"Shanty Irish."

"Krauts and Polacks. Everything has got to be clean. And dagos. Dagos put plastic on their couches. I couldn't sleep on plastic."

"Couches aren't for sleeping," Matt Schmidt said, and he was smiling.

"Funny. Ever since I split up with my wife, I can't sleep in a bed unless I'm sleeping with someone. I don't mean just screwing. I can't sleep in a bedroom. I sleep on the couch, turn the TV on, let it run all night. Odd, huh?"

Again, a moment of silence. Terry Flynn reached for a can of beer on the coffee table next to the couch where he was lying. He was lying on his stomach.

"How does your ass feel?" Matt Schmidt said.

"Want to feel it?"

"Sid Margolies told everyone."

159

"Prick. He said he wouldn't tell anyone if I gave him my Bears tickets."

"Did you?"

"Fuck, no. I'm not going to bribe a police officer. It's against the law."

"Does it hurt?"

"Sure it hurts. It may be funny to be shot in the ass but it still hurts. I told Margolies not to tell anyone about it. He was the only one I didn't trust."

"Delford goes to trial December eleventh. They cut a deal and he's going to plead down," Matt Schmidt said. "He'll do three years."

"Terrific. They ought to fry the prick," Terry Flynn said.

"The way things turned out, Jack Donovan didn't do bad—"

"Bullshit. All those guys in SAO ever want to do is get a conviction for the record and not do any work."

"We had Delford on the wrong charge on the murder thing. We were lucky to get a plea," Matt Schmidt said.

Again, they didn't speak for a moment. It was always like this after clearing a case. It was always a letdown because nothing seemed neat even though it was all over.

"How come I feel sorry for DeLeo?" Terry Flynn said at last.

"Because you don't feel sorry for Bill Conklin," Matt Schmidt said.

"He was in 'Nam twice. Poor crazy bastard. He would have made a lousy cop. We don't need any more cowboys on the department."

"I think when he got dressed up like that he thought he really was a cop. That's why he was shouting about putting us under arrest."

"Did you get heat from the Church on this?"

"Some," Matt Schmidt said. The mild word did not adequately describe the political mopping up that had followed the shootout inside St. Alma's Church. The Cardinal had been outraged and Jack Donovan was nearly transferred out of his job until Lee Horowitz explained the facts of life to Bud Halligan. Lee Horowitz had protected Jack Donovan, and that was the unlikeliest thing that happened in the matter.

Besides, as Matt Schmidt had explained to Ranallo, a detective had been wounded in an attempt to prevent the second murder of a priest.

"We calmed down the Cardinal. Remember when Margolies asked him if the Church had gotten threats? Margolies never lets go of an idea. A couple of days ago, he found out the chancery office had been threatened ten times in the past two years, individuals and institutions, and they never let us know about it."

"Why?"

"They want to keep secrets. St. Alma's had been threatened. Somebody was going to blow up the church. The usual nut note."

"How the hell did Margolies get that?"

"A friend of his. Works for the Catholic paper. But you can't tell anyone. He got Margolies in touch with a guy in the chancery office who didn't know he wasn't supposed to say anything."

"So if we had found all this out earlier—"

"We would have gone in the wrong direction," said Matthew Schmidt.

"Not that we seemed to know what we were doing in the first place," Terry Flynn said.

Matt Schmidt sat with Terry Flynn for another hour of extended small talk and then left the apartment.

Shortly after 7:00 P.M., Terry Flynn washed himself awkwardly and dressed carefully and slowly. He felt stiff-legged. The doctor had said he wouldn't be able to go back to duty until after Christmas. The idleness did not suit him, though he would have been the last to admit it.

It was cold outside. He slipped behind the wheel and eased onto a pillow he had brought down from the apartment.

He met her at Kelly's on Webster Avenue, under the El tracks. The place was bright and nearly empty and it cheered them.

"If you don't mind, I'll stand," Terry Flynn said with a smile.

"How do you feel?"

"Terrific," Terry Flynn said. "I hope it heals nice. I'd hate to have plastic surgery done."

"We shouldn't work together. We're bad luck for each other."

"Polacks," Terry Flynn said. "You're more superstitious than blacks."

"I have bad news for you," Karen Kovac said. She was sitting on a bar stool, sipping her vodka and tonic.

162

He waited.

She smiled. "Did you see the paper today?"

"No."

"Father Conklin was in the news."

"Don't let's bring that asshole up."

"He signed a contract with a New York publisher," Karen Kovac said, and she was smiling now. For two weeks after the shooting in the church, she had been shaken, both by the violence of the moment and by Terry Flynn's wounding. She had come to depend on him to be her anchor and she had been frightened to find out that Terry Flynn was as vulnerable as she was.

Terry Flynn waited.

"He's going to write a novel. About what happened. About the priest and about the priest's life. He said in the paper something like he wants to tell the truth about sex and violence in our society."

Terry Flynn grinned.

Karen Kovac laughed out loud.

"What the hell does he know about sex?" Terry Flynn said, reaching out one freckled paw to slip around Karen's waist.

"Well," Karen Kovac said, "I doubt anyone will buy it anyway."